Lina's
Redemption

This book is a work of fiction. The characters, incidents, and dialogues are products of the author's imagination and are not to be construed as real. Any references to actual events, persons, living or dead, or to real locales are intended to give the novel a sense of reality.

Lina's Redemption

Published by His Pen Publishing, LLC
Douglasville, Georgia 30135
www.hispenpublishing.com

ISBN: 978-1-944643-12-6

Library of Congress Control Number 2018940013

First Printing April 2018

This book is also available in digital eBook format

Lina's Redemption

LaCricia A'ngelle

www.hispenpublishing.com

Douglasville, Georgia

Books by LaCricia A'ngelle

Girl, Naw!
It Ain't Over

Journey to Love
Worthy of Love
The Love Child (Coming Fall 2018)

First Lady Series
Positive Deception
Lina's Redemption
SEDULOUS (Coming Summer 2018)
First Lady Blues (Coming 2019)

Stand Alone Titles
The Christmas Gift (short story)
Down by the Wishing Well (Coming 2018)
No Christmas Without You (Coming November 2018)
The Love Child (Coming 2019)

Young Adult
Sophomore Mom

This book is dedicated to you!

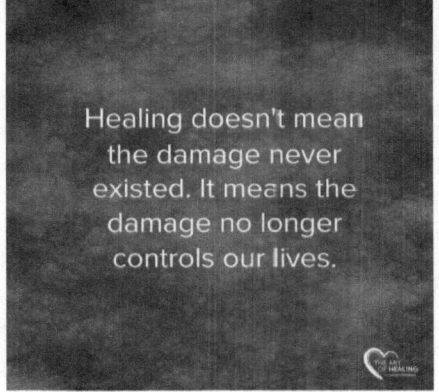

Healing doesn't mean
the damage never
existed. It means the
damage no longer
controls our lives.

Acknowledgments

To my Heavenly Father. Lord I thank You for entrusting me with such an amazing talent. I am in awe of You and Your goodness. The love you show toward me is beyond my comprehension. Father, I ask that You continue to allow me to be a light unto Your people displaying your love.

To my children, Keshonna, Larry, DeNajae, Ayonna, Gabrielle, Samantha and my little ones Landon, and baby Galler. You all keep me going. I am blessed to be your mother and Mina. Thank you for your prayers and your love. It is my desire to be a Godly example for you all to follow. Always know that I love you more than words, and that love will never fail.

To my Mama, Emma. Thank you for being my number one fan and for always encouraging me to push that literary baby out. Through the tears and frustration, you are always there to offer me encouragement and a much needed push. Thank you for being the best PR person known to man. I love you.

To my Pop, Murry. Thank you for always reminding me to continue to pray. Your love is unmatched. I love you.

To my Daddy in Heaven, Felix. There's not a day that goes by that I don't miss you. I love you always.

To my sister, Felicia. Thank you for coming through in the midnight hour in so many ways. I love you and value you and when you give me the thumbs up, I know I'm good. I love you Sissy.

To my sisters Kerri, Angie, Diane, Kim, and my sisters in love. Thank you for your encouraging words and for sharing my books with your friends. I love you all and I appreciate you.

To my nieces and nephews. I love you all so very much.

To my Bestie, Shelia. We have been on this journey a long time. I am so happy I stalked you on Myspace. (hehehe) At least that's your version. All jokes aside I know our friendship is God ordained. I'm so glad He put us in each other's life. I love you.

To my friend and mentor Jacquelin Thomas. Thank you for your wisdom and for pushing me to get the books out.

To my Pastor and First Lady Wilbur and Kim Purvis. Thank you for your love and the spiritual nourishment you so lovingly provide. I love you both. I have produced more books since I have been a part of your ministry than I have throughout my entire career. I love you both so much.

To my readers. Thank you for following my career and for supporting my books. I can't even type the word readers without acknowledging those that have read every book and pushed me to put out more. I love you all.

To Delisa, Doris, Helen, Natasha, Rena, and Tonya. Thank you for the calls, texts, and inbox messages. They mean the world to me.

I hope you'll enjoy Lina's Redemption!

Chapter One

Now let me carry you... Those words bore daggers into Lina's heart. Here she was another day, sitting on the edge of her bed, alone. She didn't know how she had the strength to step out of the car and walk away when Maxwell poured his heart out, telling her he was ready to be the man she deserved and needed, but Lina couldn't accept it. After all he'd put her through, and the way he treated her, she could never go back to him. She couldn't trust him with her heart. She would never be able to give herself to him fully out of fear of being stepped on yet again. This was not the path she wanted to take. Each moment of loneliness Lina spent she wondered if she had made the right decision. Now it was too late. She figured Maxwell had moved on with his life, and she with hers. The difference was her life was a lot emptier than she desired.

Lina stood up and made her way to the bathroom. She stared into the mirror, examining her features. Despite being HIV positive, she was otherwise the picture of health. She ate healthy meals and maintained an active lifestyle. Her skin was clear and vibrant. Long curly coils flowed past her shoulders, down her back. Without having to be told, Lina knew she was a beautiful woman. Unfortunately her beauty couldn't cure the disease taking up residence in her body.

Lina shook her head in disgust. Every time she thought of her relationship with Kaine and how a single decision to have unprotected sex completely altered her life, she grew angry. He purposely infected women with the horrible disease. She would never delight in another's demise, but she was glad Kaine was no longer alive. He didn't deserve to live.

Turning from the mirror, Lina turned on the water to fill the bathtub. She placed the back of her hand to the warm stream, testing the temperature. Her workout had been strenuous and she was looking forward to a long soak. Grabbing the Epsom salt and bubble bath from a wire rack located near the edge of her bathtub, she poured some into the stream. While the tub filled, Lina gathered her towels and phone, turning on soft jazzy tunes through her music app.

"Ooh, this is perfect," Lina said, stepping into the tub and sliding down until she was fully immersed. She closed her eyes and whispered affirmations. "I am a beautiful person both inside and out. I am fearfully and wonderfully made. I am blessed. My business is blessed. My family is blessed. I am healthy and happy. I shall live a long life." The daily affirmations had become routine for her after attending a women's empowerment conference. Reading a daily scripture and speaking the positive words helped Lina focus on the good in her life instead of dwelling on the bad things that had happened to her.

The phone rang, snapping her out of her moment of serenity. Lina rolled her eyes and looked over to the edge of the tub where her phone was resting. "Ugh, what do you want, Cheri?" Lina asked as if her best friend could hear her. She stared at the phone, contemplating whether or not to answer. The decision was made for her when the phone stopped ringing. "Thank God," she said, resting her head on the back of the tub.

Her phone played a short tune indicating an incoming text. *Call me,* the message read.

Lina rolled her eyes, wondering what was so urgent causing her friend to be diligent in her pursuits. As much as she wanted to continue her bath, Lina flipped the lever, creating a loud rustling sound as the water rushed out of the tub. With swift movements she grabbed a bath towel and wrapped herself up. Making sure the towel was secure around her body, Lina picked up her phone and dialed her friend.

Cheri answered the call on the second ring. "Hey, Lina, what are you up to?" Cheri asked.

"I was soaking in the tub trying to relax until you called and texted. Today was leg day at the gym and my trainer wore me out. What's up with you?" Lina did little to mask her irritation.

"Girl, nothing." Cheri said ignoring Lina's tone. "I was sitting here bored so I decided to give you a call. I was hoping to catch you before you went to work."

"I'm off today. I had a few floating holidays I needed to take so I decided to use the day to catch up on some freelance work. I'm thinking about taking some shots downtown and around Buckingham Fountain. If all goes well, I hope to find a few natural beauties and beaus to use in stock photos."

"It sounds like you have your plate full on your day off, might I add."

"Really," Lina laughed. "What do you consider a day off, because for me there is no such thing. I'm always on my grind making things happen."

"Yeah, okay. You can call it being on your grind if you want to," Cheri hissed.

"What would you call it?"

"I call it avoidance. I'm just saying, ever since you decided not to be with Maxwell, you've poured yourself into work. You barely go anywhere. Other than work, you don't do much."

"Stop trippin', Cheri. Nothing has changed. You are being dramatic for no reason. I still go out and do stuff. Didn't we go to the movies last weekend?"

"I guess when I see you I owe you a trophy because you went to the movies for the first time in close to a year. On second thought, the reason you love working all the time might have to do with that fine boss of yours. What's his name? Charles Davenport?" Cheri snapped her fingers, "Yep that's it, Mr. Davenport. Honey, if I had a daily dose of eye candy to enjoy, I wouldn't be trying to miss out on that either. You need to drop the shy act and go ahead and get that man. How long have you worked for him?"

"Three years, and yes Mr. Davenport is fine, but I'm not going there."

"Why not?"

"Let's see. Perhaps it's because he's my boss. Or maybe it's because I'm HIV positive. Did you forget that? This shop is closed for good."

"Why do you always have to bring up your medical condition? HIV is not the end of the world. Besides, yours is managed and you're healthier than most of the people I know. You are not doomed to a life of obscurity, and you don't have to live the rest of your life as an old maid."

Lina rolled her eyes and switched her phone to the

other ear. "That's easy for you to say, Cheri. You don't live my life. I'm good. Trust me, I'm enjoying life despite the fact I don't have a man. Not everybody is meant to be in a relationship."

"If telling yourself that is what keeps you warm at night, who am I to try to talk some sense into you. Do your thing girl. Just know God has more for you than what you can see."

"I hear you." Lina took a seat on the edge of the tub. The phone call was lasting much longer than she had anticipated. She had things to do and she knew if she allowed Cheri to continue they would be on the phone another hour. "Cheri, I'll have to talk to you later. I'm losing daylight and I like to get some shots when the sun is just right."

"I understand. I won't hold you up any longer." Cheri paused for a moment. "Lina, I want the best for you. Only God knows what's best for any of us. I didn't mean any harm. I want my best friend to be happy."

"That's the whole point, Cheri. I *am* happy. Now let me get off this phone. Talk to you later, girl."

Lina pulled the phone away from her ear and touched the end button. She got up from the tub and placed her phone on the vanity. Everything she said to Cheri sounded good in theory but she knew Cheri didn't buy it any more than she did herself. What were the odds Cheri would call her and pretty much have the same conversation she herself had in the recesses of her mind?

Cheri's phone call lasted long enough that Lina didn't have to continue toweling off. She went into her bedroom and put on the clothes she had laid out for herself. Once she was dressed and ready to go, she looked up and tilted her head. She spoke softly but with all sincerity, "If there is a man for me out there, you're going to have to bring him to me."

Chapter Two

The temperature in downtown Chicago was a pleasant seventy degrees. A gentle breeze flowed through Lina's curly tresses as she captured shots of Buckingham Fountain, Crown Fountain, and Cloud Gate. Most tourists and city natives referred to Cloud Gate as *the bean* because of its kidney bean shape. Lina admired it, not only for its dynamic shape, but also because of its unique surface. She captured images of herself with her camera through the reflection of the structure.

The Friday afternoon crowd grew at a steady pace. Lina attributed it to the nice weather and spring fever. Chicago had suffered a bitter winter with temperatures plummeting to thirty degrees below zero at times. Now that the pleasant May temperatures had arrived people were starting to get out to enjoy Grant Park. Taking a seat on the grass, Lina decided to people watch for a little while, hoping to find some interesting subjects to add to her portfolio. She reached into her camera bag and checked for her release forms and business cards. Everything was in place.

Holding her camera firmly, Lina noticed a man playing with a toddler. She watched as he ran around chasing the little boy on the grass. Huge smiles could be seen on both their faces as the man gently tossed the child in the air and caught him. She gingerly approached them and introduced herself, extending her business card to him. With his permission and signed release, she snapped away, capturing the precious moment.

"Go, Mama," a young girl called out as she stood on the sidelines cheering on a woman who appeared to be in her thirties turning cartwheels.

This will make some great action shots, she thought. With their permission, she snapped multiple pictures. The daughter joined her mother, performing a few flips of her own. Lina continued to photograph random scenes for the next hour.

Lina was preparing to wrap things up when she noticed a woman standing near the fountain. She was beautiful. Her honey complexion was radiant beneath a fuchsia, off the shoulder blouse and navy blue cropped slacks that stopped at the ankle. The fountain's seahorses provided the perfect backdrop for a photo. Not wanting to miss the opportunity, she approached the woman.

"Hi, my name is Lina. I'm a freelance photographer taking random photos today." Lina handed the woman her business card. "I was wondering if you would allow me to photograph you and the fountain."

"What kind of pictures are you trying to take? I'm not into that kinky stuff."

Stifling a laugh, Lina turned her camera so the woman could see the other pictures she had taken earlier. "Trust me, the pictures are not at all risqué. If you agree, I'll provide you with a digital photo package which will include all the photos I shoot of you. All I need is your permission and a signed release." She pulled the form out of her bag.

The woman examined the form closely. "Okay, I'll do it

as long as I get to see every picture you take when you're done. You also have to promise not to Photoshop my picture into some crazy setting. By the way, my name is Amirah."

"It's nice to meet you, Amirah and showing you the pictures won't be a problem." Lina handed the woman a pen to complete the form. When she was done, Lina placed the form in her bag and positioned Amirah near the seahorses. "I want you to act normal for these first shots. Pretend like I'm not here. Lina snapped away. "You're such a natural. You should consider modeling."

"That's sweet of you but I don't have time for modeling. I stay busy."

Adjusting her camera, Lina said, "For this next set of pictures, I want you to smile and look at the camera." *Click, click, click.* The shutter sounded like music to Lina as she captured each picture. She noticed Amirah's smile grew when her eyes fell on something behind Lina.

"There's my hubby," she waved her hand, beckoning him over. "Can he get in these pictures too? We need some updated pics."

"Sure," Lina said, turning to see who Amirah was speaking of. "Maxwell," Lina said, with hesitation. She looked down and noticed the gold band on his left hand.

"Hello, Lina."

Amirah stepped over to Maxwell and took his hand. She looked at their odd expressions. "You two know each other?" she asked with furrowed eyebrows.

Maxwell kissed his wife's cheek. "Lina used to attend the church, baby. We haven't seen each other in quite a while."

"Oh, okay," Amirah replied, unconvinced.

"I see you're still taking pictures," Maxwell said to Lina. Lina held up her camera.

"Yes, she is. Now come over here so she can take some of us together." Amirah interjected, preventing further conversation between Maxwell and Lina.

Maxwell complied with his wife's wishes and stood near the fountain, pulling her into his arms.

Lina continued the photo shoot, ignoring the knot that had formed in her belly. She'd wondered how she would feel if she ever saw Maxwell in person. However, she didn't plan on seeing him with a wife. Lina finished the shoot and walked over to the couple. She had to admit they looked good together. They loved each other and the camera captured it beautifully. As promised, she turned the camera, allowing Amirah to view the pictures."

Amirah threw one arm over Lina's shoulder and hugged her. "Wow. These pictures are amazing. I'm so glad I agreed to do this. Thank you so much."

"I told you, you're a natural, and you and Maxwell look great together. I'll email you the photos in about a week."

"Thank you again." Amirah jumped in Maxwell's arms and kissed him.

Once he was free from her embrace, Maxwell turned to Lina and extended his hand. "Thank you for the impromptu photo shoot. Amirah has been trying to get some photos of us done for a while. God's timing is perfect. It was good seeing you, Lina."

Shaking his hand quickly, Lina nodded. "You're more than welcome. His timing is perfect indeed. It was good seeing you, too. Take care." Lina placed the camera in her bag and turned and walked away.

Chapter Three

Keys jingled in Lina's trembling hand, duplicating the sound of Christmas bells. Shallow breaths caused her chest to rise and fall rapidly. She had coached herself over the past two years on how to behave should she ever see Maxwell again. Overall, she had done good but she couldn't hide the shock of finding out he was married.

Lina put the key in the ignition and turned the car on. She couldn't get away from the park fast enough. Her mind easily drifted back to Maxwell and Amirah. She hated to admit how happy they looked. Over the years she had photographed hundreds of couples. She could tell when there was genuine love as opposed to someone faking it for the camera. Lina pressed her back into the seat. She gripped the steering wheel tightly and took a deep breath, resigning herself to the fact Maxwell had continued his life without her.

As badly as she wanted to forget about Maxwell and everything going on with him, Lina couldn't let it go. She pulled her phone out of her pocket and selected Cheri's number from the list of recent calls. She put the call on speaker and waited for her friend to answer.

"Hello," Cheri answered, sounding a bit distracted.

"Where are you? We need to talk," Lina belted out the words in a panicked tone.

"Lina? What's going on? Are you okay?" Cheri asked, giving Lina her full attention.

"Calm down. I didn't mean to alarm you. I do need to see you though, as soon as possible. This is urgent. Can you meet me at Giordano's on Randolph?"

"I'm still at the office. I have some stuff I have to wrap up first, but I can meet you in about thirty minutes. Are you going to tell me what it is that has you so upset?"

"I'll tell you when I see you. I can't tell you over the phone it has to be in person. I'll see you at the restaurant." Lina disconnected the call quickly and turned her focus back to the downtown traffic. She applied more pressure to the gas pedal and maneuvered in and out of the busy lanes.

Lina arrived at the world renown pizza restaurant in fifteen minutes. She pulled into the parking lot and parked in the first available space. Peering around the parking lot she looked for Cheri's vehicle, despite knowing her friend wouldn't be there yet. She was overly anxious and didn't like that feeling. Lina looked at her watch and then checked the time on her phone. She knew it was ridiculous, but she didn't know what else to do with herself. Her heart rate and breathing increased, displaying the obvious anxiety she was feeling. "Calm down, Lina," she spoke to herself aloud and took several deep breaths. She closed her eyes and shifted her focus from Maxwell and Amirah in an effort to release the mounting stress.

The beep of a horn startled her. She opened her eyes and turned her head in the direction of the sound. Cheri sat in the vehicle next to her, waving. Lina grabbed her purse and removed her keys from the ignition. She and Cheri simultaneously exited their vehicles and greeted one another with a hug.

"Girl, what's going on? If I wasn't trippin' I would say you're shaking." Cheri observed her friend with concern etched across her face.

"Let's get inside. You need to be sitting down when I tell you what happened to me today." Lina moved in front of Cheri and approached the entrance of the restaurant.

A handsome man appearing to be in his early thirties held the door open for the ladies and scanned their bodies.

"Ugh," Lina said loud enough for him to hear her. The man dropped his head and released the door after they were both inside.

"Girl, what is your problem? Why were you so mean to that man?"

"Men like him get on my nerves. Gawking at us like we were prime rib or something. They make me sick. He was practically drooling and it wasn't from anything the restaurant was serving."

"Okay, you're trippin' for real, Lina. I don't mind receiving adoration from the male species. You think I go through all the trouble of fixing myself up every day for men not to notice. That's crazy."

"Two please," Lina spoke kindly to the hostess. The woman grabbed two menus, escorted them to the center of the restaurant, and seated them at a table. The server was at their table before the hostess could step away. He took their drink orders and promised to return quickly.

"Are you ready to tell me what's going on now, or are you going to keep stalling?" Cheri looked at her friend with a raised eyebrow.

"Hold up a second, Cheri. I'm going to tell you. I didn't have you come all the way here for nothing. Can we please at least order first? I'm starved. Let's get a deep dish, my treat."

Cheri rolled her eyes at her friend before turning her attention to the menu. "I think I want a salad."

"Then we'll get both. I know you're not going to make me eat a whole pizza by myself."

The server returned to the table and placed a cup of water with a lemon wedge anchored on the side in front of Lina. Next, he put a Pepsi in front of Cheri. Cheri pulled the paper wrapping off the straw he provided and placed it inside the cup. Taking a long sip, she let out a soft moan.

Lina focused her attention on the server. "We'll have the Chicago deep dish, but I want to substitute the pepperoni for sausage. Also, please give us a Caesar salad." The server nodded and stepped away from the table.

Cheri's eyes bore into Lina. Lina accepted the unspoken prompt. "You'll never guess who I saw today," Lina said.

"Lina, you've stalled long enough. I'm not in the mood for a round of guessing games. Stop playing and tell me what's going on."

"Fine, Cheri. I told you I was going to take pictures at Grant Park today. Well I did. One of the people I photographed was a beautiful woman. I mean I have to give the sistah credit, she was gorgeous. Anyway, during my shoot with her, her husband came up and she asked if he could be included in the picture. Of course, I said yes. Girl, you won't believe who her husband was."

"Who? A celebrity?" Cheri asked in eager anticipation.

"I wish it was a celebrity, then I wouldn't be feeling all crazy. Cheri, it was Maxwell."

Cheri gasped and covered her mouth with her hand. She slowly lowered her hand. With wide eyes she stared at her friend. "Your Maxwell? Maxwell Lee?"

"The one and only."

"Oh, my God. Girl, what did you do? I would have died right there."

"Now you see why I needed you to meet me."

Cheri took another sip of her Pepsi and sat back in her chair with her arms across the table. She watched as Lina squeezed the lemon juice into her water and stirred the water with her straw. "What did you do?"

"Nothing, okay. I did nothing. His wife noticed we were looking at each other with odd expressions, so naturally she asked if we knew each other. Before I could say anything, he told her I used to attend the church a while ago."

"Wow. He introduced you as a former church member? That's cold."

"Tell me about it. I wasn't trying to cause mess between them, so I went along with it. I took their pictures the same as I would anyone else. That wasn't even the hardest part though. The hard part was seeing their love for each other while I took the pictures. He looked at her like she was God's gift."

"Dang, Lina. I'm sorry, girl." Cheri stretched her arm across the table and placed it on top of her friend's hand. She gently rubbed the back of Lina's hand before pulling her arm back.

"When Maxwell showed up at my job a couple years ago telling me all that stuff about him seeing the light," Lina raised her hands with her palms up in illustration, "he never looked at me the way he did her. It just goes to show, he didn't really want me. He was going to settle for me because Minister Lee," she used her fingers to make air quotes when she said Minister Lee, "wanted to do the right thing. I don't want to be the right thing for a man. I want to be the love of his life. That's how Maxwell looked at Amirah. Like she was the love of his life. If a man can't look at me like that, then I'd rather stay single."

The server returned and placed the pizza and salad on the table. He sat small plates in front of both of them, leaving them to serve themselves. As quickly as he appeared, he left again.

Cheri used the spatula to select a slice of the thick, gooey pizza. She placed the pizza on her plate and handed Lina the spatula to serve herself. "Look at it like this. You didn't want Maxwell. He wasn't the man for you. You knew it and I'm pretty sure, deep down inside he knew he had ruined any chance of getting you back. He has moved on. Fine. God bless him, but please know, God is not going to give him someone to love and not do the same for you. Despite what you have going on in your body."

"I wish I could believe you, Cheri. I really do."

"You can believe me, Lina. You need to choose to believe it. When you truly open your heart, the right man will come in and he will love you for the woman you are. You'll see. It won't be like this forever." Cheri took her fork and pulled off the tip of her pizza slice. She placed it in her mouth and closed her eyes once again. "Ooh wee, this is so good. I'm glad you convinced me to have the pizza. She looked down at the salad sitting on the table and pointed at it with her fork. "Instead of that ole sad looking salad."

Lina couldn't help but to laugh at her best friend. She was happy for the distraction. While she savored every bite of her pizza she pondered Cheri's words. Maybe she did deserve to be loved. Perhaps there could be a man out there who would love her. She made a mental note to look up people online who had found love after being diagnosed with HIV. She was sure there were some examples out there somewhere.

"Enough about me, Cheri. Tell me about you and David. Is he being good to you?"

A smile instantly creased Cheri's lips. She didn't mind talking about her boyfriend. He was her favorite topic of conversation. "Can you believe we have been together for over a year? I can't lie, every day is like day one. I'm still trying to impress him, and he's still trying to impress me."

"After all this time, the two of you are still not comfortable in your relationship?" Lina asked.

"I'm not saying we're not comfortable. What I mean about us still trying to impress each other is he still goes out of his way to do nice things for me that will make me happy and I do the same for him. We love each other."

"When you have love, you can overcome a lot. When the love is real that is," Lina said.

Chapter Four

Lina hooked her camera up to the computer and downloaded the pictures she shot downtown. She admired her work and was grateful for the gift of photography and a good eye. She scanned the photos and lingered on the photo of the father and son. She clicked on the picture of the mother and daughter next before stopping on a picture of Maxwell and Amirah. She was over the shock of his marriage. It's not like she wanted him. Had she wanted him, she would have had him. It was her choice to walk away and she didn't regret it despite the loneliness she felt.

Looking at the pictures, she felt a deep longing inside—not for Maxwell, but for the entire scene that played out before her. The parents with their children and the couples. She hated to admit it, but she wanted what they all had. A relationship. She thought of her parents and siblings. They were all living their lives and they were happy. She loved her nephew who was also her godson deeply but it wasn't the same as having a child of her own. She longed to be a wife and a mother, to have someone look upon her with the love and adoration she saw portrayed in the photos she had taken.

Lina saved the photos to her computer and shut down the device. No longer would she spend the day dwelling on what she didn't have and what she felt she was missing out on. It wasn't worth the time or effort she was putting into it. Lina rose from her computer and walked over to the kitchen. She pulled the box of leftover pizza from the fridge and placed a slice on a pan and stuck it in the oven. She was hungry, but not starving, so she preferred to heat her meal in the oven as opposed to the microwave.

While her pizza was heating up she stepped over to the living room and turned on the television. She pressed the button that gave her access to the on-demand programs and searched for her favorite shows. Lina loved to watch comedies. She felt laughter was her best medicine. She wasn't in the mood to watch some love story that gave viewers unrealistic expectations. She also didn't want to see anyone being killed in a suspense thriller, or to get deep into her feelings with a drama. Reality television was a definite no for her, so comedy would be her sweet spot for the day.

Lina threw her head back as she laughed at the actors running through the house chasing a pet pig. Why in the world someone would choose a barnyard animal as a pet was beyond her understanding. Lina had tried to have a pet as a teen but she couldn't deal with the responsibility that came along with it. She always had a difficult time training puppies and her mother was allergic to cats so they were out of the question.

A commercial for dog food came on and Lina couldn't help but to gush at the small furry dog that looked like he was smiling at the woman in the commercial. "Maybe that's what I need, a dog," she said aloud. Although it didn't work out when she was younger, she was much older and could afford to send the dog for training and have someone else housebreak it. She looked around her empty apartment. She wanted a companion even if it was a four-legged one.

"I can't believe I'm seriously considering this," Lina said as she walked into the kitchen and retrieved her pizza from the oven. "I'm gonna get a dog." Several of her coworkers had dogs and they often spoke about the bond they had with their pets. They told her their pets loved them unconditionally. Unconditional love was exactly what she needed.

Lina placed the pizza on a plate and walked back into the living room. For the first time in a while, she had something to look forward to. Her job had been very rewarding with the constant travel and all the perks that came along with her position. She would have to find a good boarder to keep her pet when she was away on assignment but she knew she could make it work.

The phone rang as she was finishing up her meal. She smiled when she saw her nephew's image displayed on the screen. She used his picture as her sister, Zarion's, contact photo.

"What's up, Z?"

"Girl, what are you up to? I know you're not that excited to talk to me," Zarion replied.

"Yes, I am," Lina said in a soft, innocent tone. "I love hearing from my sister. How's my nephew?"

"Finally, the truth. It's not me you're crazy about. It's this spoiled little boy I gave birth to. You're not slick."

"Okay, you got me. I'll admit it. I'm a sucker for Daniel. He's the sweetest baby in the whole wide world, and I can't get enough of him. I need to book a flight and come to see him."

"He's getting so big, Lina. I don't know what to do with

him. He's into everything. When they said terrible two's, they weren't lying. As a matter of fact, you can come see him, and take his little bad butt back with you when you leave, too."

"Don't tempt me, Z. I will do it. He can't be that bad."

"Danny, no!" Zarion yelled just before Lina heard a crash in the background. There was some shuffling before her sister returned to the phone.

"Yeah, come on get this little boy. Can you be here today?"

"What happened? I heard you yelling and a crash. Is he okay?"

"He pulled my plant down off the stand. There's dirt everywhere. I told you he was bad. His little butt is always into stuff. I can barely keep up with him."

"I don't mean to laugh, but I can imagine what that scene looks like." Lina continued to laugh until Zarion interrupted her.

"Go ahead and laugh all you want. I bet you wouldn't be laughing if it was your camera he knocked over instead of a plant."

"That's not even funny, Z. You know my camera is my money maker. Don't be messing with my money. I don't play those kind of games." Lina paused for a moment. "Guess what, Z."

"What's up, baby sis?"

"I've decided to get a dog."

"A dog? What on earth are you going to do with a dog? You couldn't handle a dog when we lived at home with Mama and Daddy."

"I was a kid then. I can handle it now. It'll be nice to have something else in the apartment breathing other than me."

"If that's what you want to do, I say go for it. I'm not going to be the one to dash your dreams."

"Thank you. Besides, I think it's going to be a good thing.

"Whatever makes you happy, Lina, but I will say this. You thought it was funny when Daniel knocked over my plant, just wait until you get a dog. You'll have a lot more than a plant to worry about."

"You can't deter me. Plus, I'm sending it to obedience training before I bring it home. I'll have the best little doggie. You'll see."

"I forgot you were balling. Go head on, Miss Big Shot Photographer. Do you, boo."

Lina continued to chat with her sister for a little more than a half hour before ending their call. It always felt good talking to her family, but she had no desire to move back home to Durham. She opened up the search app on her phone and looked up small dogs. It was time for her to find her fur baby.

Chapter Five

Loose papers shifted on Charles' desk as he paced the length of his office. He had worked for the company for over eight years, accepting the job straight out of college. It was hard for him to believe his time at *About Us* magazine was ending. He'd received a promotion from Watchman Journal, their parent company. Watchman Journal expected him to start his new position at the beginning of the month, which only gave him two weeks to complete the transition. Since everything had been finalized, it was time to alert his staff. His replacement was selected and the staff at Watchman Journal was aware of the upcoming change. Shifting his stance, Charles peered through his glass wall at the small staff he managed as they prepared to start their work day.

Lina entered the room, displaying the beautiful smile he had become accustomed to seeing. Although he'd never mentioned it to her, her presence made each day more meaningful. He enjoyed when they had assignments requiring them to travel to exotic locations. It was during those trips when he developed feelings that exceeded those of a manager and employee. When he was home alone he thought about her. He visualized her face and replayed their time together, allowing her laughter to fill his heart and mind. Charles knew he would miss her most of all. He considered Lina his *work wife* even though, according to the company's rules, a relationship between them was strictly prohibited.

Once everyone had arrived and was seated, Charles stepped out of his office. He drew everyone's attention and asked them to meet with him in the boardroom. The long mahogany desk in the boardroom was surrounded by twenty black leather executive chairs. His staff of eight was able to assemble comfortably with room to spare.

"What's going on?" Charles' secretary, Elizabeth, asked in response to the inquiries she received from her coworkers.

"Come on in and have a seat," Charles instructed, ignoring her question. He extended his hand to usher the staff into the room. Once everyone was seated, he took the position at the head of the table. Choosing not to sit along with the staff, he continued to stand. "As you all know, I'm not big on sending emails, especially for things I deem as extremely important. I'm a hands-on, face to face guy." He paused for reactions from the staff before continuing. "We all have worked together for quite some time and I feel it's important for me to talk to you collectively." He noticed the look of concern displayed on the faces of some of the staff. "Don't worry, no one's losing their job." He waited for them to relax in their seats before he continued. "There is, however, going to be a major change in this office. I have accepted the position of Vice President of Marketing for our parent company. I will be moving into my new position the first of the month."

A loud sigh was heard throughout the room as the staff listened with great intent to Charles outline the details of the transition. The members of the eight-person team appeared to have different reactions. Some appeared sad at the news, while others displayed expressions of confusion and indifference.

Donald, a man in his mid-twenties, sat at the end of the table with a smirk on his face. He never cared much for Charles and was happy to hear of his imminent departure. No longer would he have to put up with Charles challenging everything he did. Donald also knew from a friend in human resources Charles had recommended he be terminated on at least one occasion.

Rubbing her shoulders and arms as if she was fighting off a bitter cold, Lina sat stoic. She didn't know what the change would mean for her since Charles had personally selected her for the position of staff photographer. She'd enjoyed an entertaining, lucrative lifestyle traveling and doing what she loved most, taking pictures. Since taking on the position at *About Us* her income had grown steadily and rapidly. The most enjoyable part was traveling with Charles on several of the assignments. His change in position could easily cause a drastic change for her as well.

As if he'd read her thoughts, Charles said, "I want you all to know, no matter what position you are currently in, your jobs are secure. I've been assured my change will not affect any of you. You each do an excellent job. Both the company and I are appreciative of your efforts." Charles made eye contact with Lina before diverting his eyes. Following his announcement, he saw several team members visually relax.

Donald raised his right hand, appointing himself as the designated spokesman for the group. With his left hand he drummed his fingers on the table, being sure to be extra distractive. He intensified his level of disrespect by clearing his throat.

Charles directed his attention to Donald and paused before acknowledging his attention seeking antics. "What is it, Donald?"

In a condescending tone, Donald said, "Look here, Mr. Davenport. I understand everything you're saying and all." He paused and stood, folding his arms. He held his stance as if he and Charles were going to square off in a fight. "Congratulations on your promotion. However, I'm sure I'm not the only one in this room who realizes you left out some important information. I didn't hear you mention who's taking over your position. I believe we have a right to know who we'll be working with." Donald extended his arms to the members of the team for support.

A few of the team members nodded in agreement.

Charles' jaw tightened. Donald was trying his patience. Who did he think he was? It was one thing to ask a question but he didn't have to do it in such a disrespectful way? The two men had clashed from the moment Donald joined Charles' team. He was transferred from a different department due to his failure to cooperate with the team leader. After hearing the report, Charles felt Donald should have been terminated. An idea immediately shot down by the company executives. He was told Donald was excellent at his job and his skill level was unmatched by his co-workers. Almost immediately, Charles also discovered Donald was a master manipulator. He knew how far to go in order to keep his job.

"I realize you all may be wondering who your new team leader will be. In all fairness I feel it is most appropriate for him to introduce himself. I can tell you he was hired from outside the company and his name is Jackson Parks.

Jackson is scheduled to be here in a few days. The two of us will work side by side until the end of the month, when he will take over."

"Figures they would hire someone from outside the company," Donald retorted. "As if we don't have employees well qualified to take the position." Donald's remarks caused an unrest among the team. The low hum of protest escalated into all out rebellion.

Charles raised his palms to the staff, regaining control of the meeting. "I understand you may be frustrated, but this is beyond all of our control. The company has made their decision. I urge you to keep an open mind and to give Jackson your full support." Having finished his discussion concerning the transition, Charles took a seat at the table and shifted gears. "I know it's pretty early but since we're already gathered, let's go ahead and have our morning meeting."

Chapter Six

Lina dashed across the room to silence the ringing phone. She banged her foot on the end table, sending a surge of pain throughout her body. "Ouch!" Grabbing her foot, she hopped the remaining distance. Lina squeezed her eyes tight, hoping the action would diminish the throbbing. Taking a deep breath, she pressed accept on her phone.

"Fairweather Photography, this is Lina."

"Lina, hi. This is Maxwell. Maxwell Lee."

She stared at the phone in disbelief. This was a call Lina never expected to receive, especially given Maxwell's marital status. Making her way to the couch with an exaggerated limp, she attempted to sound unbothered. "You don't have to be formal. I know who you are. I recognized your voice." Taking a seat on the couch, she continued to massage her ailing foot. "If you're calling about the pictures, I emailed the files to your wife earlier this week. I included a copyright release so she can have them printed wherever she chooses."

"Yes, I saw the pictures. They were amazing. You did a phenomenal job. Not that I had any doubts." Maxwell's words trailed off. Several breaths passed between them before he continued. "That's not the reason I'm calling."

"It's not? Then why *are* you calling?" Lina struggled to keep her frustration at bay. She didn't want to come across as rude, but if not for the pictures she felt the married, preacherman had no reason to call her.

"You still like to get straight to the point, I see." Maxwell cleared his throat. "I was calling to check on you. You know, to see how you're doing. We haven't communicated in a long time. I've thought about you often."

"I'm doing just fine," Lina said with a sharper tone than she planned. "I must admit, I'm still confused by your call. Why did you feel the need to call to check on me?"

"I can imagine it was awkward finding out I was married the way you did. To make matters worse, you were put in a position to take photos of me and my wife. I couldn't talk to you then, so I thought today might be a good day to call you. I suppose I should have asked if you were in the middle of something."

"Your timing is fine; however, I don't see the necessity of your call. I'm happy you've moved on with your life. You don't owe me an explanation for the decisions you make. You're entitled to live your life any way you choose." Lina realized there was even more of a bite in her tone. "I'm sorry. That sounded a bit harsh didn't it?"

"Yeah, it did," Maxwell admitted. "But it's cool, I understand."

"I appreciate your understanding, but I know it wasn't cool." Lina closed her eyes and took a breath. Hearing Maxwell's voice caused her heart to yearn. The reality of his marriage intensified the pain of loneliness she felt. Her moment of silence lasted longer than she realized. The faint sound of Maxwell calling her name evolved into what sounded like a shout.

"Lina. Are you there? Is everything okay?" Maxwell asked concerned.

"I'm fine. I was thinking about something." Each moment of the phone call felt like torture. Lina had to end it. "Maxwell, I appreciate your call, but I need to get back to work. I'm happy to know you found someone, and I wish you the best."

"Wait, Lina. Before you hang up, I pray the Lord will bless you as well. I also want to extend an invitation to you. Great things are happening at Christ the True Vine. The vision is coming to pass in a mighty way. I'd love for you to stop by sometime."

"Thanks, but no thanks, Maxwell. Have a good day." Lina disconnected the call before Maxwell could offer a rebuttal. How dare he invite her to his church with his wife. The knot in her belly that had remained since seeing him at Grant Park was now gone. Maxwell was the same insensitive jerk he'd always been. For the first time since Lina stepped out of his vehicle more than two years ago refusing his plea to give him another chance, Lina knew she'd made the right decision.

Fueled with anger, Lina leaped from the couch with a mind to go to her computer and delete the photos she'd taken of Maxwell and his wife. Her foot throbbed, reminding her of her injury. She fell back on the couch and muttered a curse. "Ugh, I can't stand you Maxwell Lee. I hope I never hear your voice or see your stupid face again."

Chapter Seven

Balloons and well wishes filled the offices of *About Us* magazine. Tables piled high with finger foods and desserts lined the walls of the breakroom. Charles strolled through the familiar setting with mixed emotions. He looked forward to his new position, but it came at the cost of losing the staff he had grown to love. Many of the members of his team had been handpicked and hired by him.

One by one, team members took time out to offer him parting words of encouragement, and their sentiments. Charles constantly looked at his watch followed by a glance at the entrance of the office. Donald entered Charles' office and leaned against the doorframe.

"She's not coming in today," Donald said in a mocking tone.

"Excuse me?" Charles retorted, folding his arms across his chest.

"Man, chill out. You don't have to get all defensive. I know what's up even if she doesn't. You keep strolling through the office, and I've seen you watching the door. I'm not stupid. I know who you're looking for. Lina's not here today, and in case you're wondering, she's not coming in. Jackson sent her out on assignment. Didn't you get the email? We all received it."

Refusing to be outdone, Charles sat up straighter in his

seat. "I must have overlooked the email. Thanks for letting me know. I was hoping to say farewell to each of you. I'll shoot her an email."

The men engaged in a non-verbal standoff. Charles broke the silence. "Is there anything else you need, Donald? If not, I have some things I need to take care of."

"That's cool, I was done." Donald turned to leave. "Congrats again on your new position. Don't forget about us over here," he called out over his shoulder.

"Yeah, thanks." Using his first two fingers, Charles gave Donald a salute.

Relaxing back in his chair, Charles folded his hands together and placed his thumbs under his chin. A slight frown creased his forehead. For the sake of making the transition as smooth as possible, Jackson had taken on the responsibility of assigning tasks to the team members. Charles was confident in Jackson's abilities to run things. He didn't feel the need to micromanage his successor. Several of the emails Jackson sent had been disregarded by Charles. Now he wished he had paid a bit more attention. Not being able to say goodbye to Lina cast an unwanted shadow on his day.

Elizabeth, Charles' secretary, entered his office and closed the door behind her. She walked over and took a seat in the chair in front of his desk. Crossing her legs, she revealed a slender, shapely thigh. She folded her hands together and allowed them to rest on her knee.

Charles watched her actions with boredom. He had worked with Elizabeth for several years and had become numb to her advances. She'd roamed the floors of the office like a tantalizing seductress which was a complete turn-off for him. Charles cleared his throat, prompting her to get on with the purpose for her visit.

She placed her hand on the back of her neck and tossed the long wavy weave she was sporting. "Charles, we're going to miss you around here," she began. "Jackson seems okay, but he's a bit uptight. The vibe in this office will be different for sure."

He watched her animated movements. Elizabeth was practically cooing the words from her lips.

"I just have one question for you, Charles."

"What's your question, Elizabeth?" Charles glanced at his watch. He wanted her to know his interest in the conversation was lacking, without being overly disrespectful.

"You're going to be a powerful man in that new position of yours. I've worked for you for a while and I've always done a great job. You said so yourself during my evaluations. I want to know why you chose not to take me with you. I'm sure you're going to have an admin assistant in your new position. Why not pick me, someone you know quite well?"

Charles considered her words. She was right, he did know her. The truth of the matter is he knew her too well. Charles had consulted with his colleagues on multiple occasions on how well the men in management positions at *About Us* knew her. Many of them knew her in the biblical sense of the word. Charles was not interested in carrying on the tradition by taking her with him. He was glad to be getting away from her.

Keeping his tone as neutral as possible, Charles gave her a flat smile and placed his hands on top of the desk. "I'm glad you've enjoyed working with me, Elizabeth. I would have considered bringing you on board at Watchman

Journal but the staff is already in place over there. I wanted to extend to them the same courtesy I extended to my team by not uprooting anyone from their job. I'm sure you'll find a way to get into a routine with Jackson that you're comfortable with. Everything is going to work out. You'll see. Now if you'll excuse me, I need to wrap some things up."

Charles spoke with finality. Elizabeth could see there was no need for rebuttal when Charles turned his attention from her back to his computer screen. She nodded before rising to leave. She didn't bother to offer him well wishes as she knew there was nothing left to be said.

The rest of the work day was spent with various team members coming in to offer their goodbyes to Charles. At one point it felt more like visitation at a funeral home, than a last day of work. Some team members reminisced over moments that had occurred while working for him. Others talked about what it was like to work for him and how much they would miss him. As the clock neared the four o'clock hour, Charles was wiped out. He had tied up every loose end possible and exhaustion was starting to set in. There was no need to prolong the inevitable.

He checked over his office one last time, going through each drawer and looking on each shelf to make sure he hadn't left anything behind. Charles moved throughout the office, saying final goodbyes to the team members. He looked over at Lina's desk, committing her smile to memory even though her seat was empty. It was time for him to move forward. His only regret was leaving Lina behind.

Chapter Eight

"I'm so glad you convinced me to come with you and David today. The weather is beautiful and this food is delicious." Lina spoke to Cheri between bites of her Italian beef sandwich.

"Girl, I told you, The Taste be poppin'. You might even find you a man out here. God knows there are plenty to choose from.

The Taste of Chicago Festival had been a favorite of Lina's since moving to Chicago. The aroma from the different foods prepared by the vendors was intoxicating. Although she worked hard to stay healthy and to keep her figure together, Lina allowed herself a temporary pass to overindulge at the annual July event. It was also the rare occasion where she didn't have her camera with her. If she found a subject worth capturing, she did so with the camera on her phone.

"They can keep the men, I'm here for the food. The only thing I'm trying to kiss right now is this bun," Lina joked as she took another bite from her sandwich.

"Yeah, but the bun won't kiss you back and pretty soon, it'll be gone."

The ladies united in robust laughter. David walked up carrying three soft drinks. He gave one to each of the ladies before taking a gulp from the one remaining in his hand.

"I don't know why you like coming to this overpriced thing. I could probably take you to each of these restaurants and it would cost less than what they charge for a bite here. I just spent close to twenty dollars on these three drinks," David complained.

"Babe, stop being cheap. It's not like we do this every day. Besides, it makes me happy. You do want me to be happy, don't you?" Cheri lowered her voice and batted her eyes.

David let out a nervous giggle. "Of course, I want you to be happy. It's cool. What do you want to do next?" he asked, sounding like a genie in the bottle eager to grant Cheri's wishes.

Lina observed the exchange before diverting her attention elsewhere. This was an example of why she didn't like to go places with Cheri and David. She didn't care for the feeling of being the third wheel. She also didn't like putting her best friend in a position of having to divide her attention.

"I'll be back," Lina said, using her index finger to point in the direction of the restroom.

"We'll more than likely move on from here," Cheri warned.

"No problem. I'll call and see where you are when I head back this way."

Lina had no intentions of going to the restroom. She used the excuse to give Cheri and David some alone time. Being single, she was accustomed to going places alone and she had no problem entertaining herself. Lina walked several paces when she noticed her shoe was untied. She moved from the flow of foot traffic to tie her shoe. Feeling secure in her location, she bent down to tie her shoe.

"Whoa," a man called out as he practically fell over her.

"Dang, watch where you're going." Lina stood quickly with a frown.

"Excuse...," the man turned and stopped mid-sentence. "Lina."

"You have got to be kidding me," Lina said with a laugh. All her anger had evaporated. "Charles, what are you doing here?"

"I'm out here getting my grub on, just like everybody else. How have you been?" Charles pulled Lina into an embrace, leaving no room for protest.

"I've been good," Lina replied, stepping back from him.

"It's hard to believe it's been two months already. I wasn't sure I'd ever get to see you again." Charles smiled as he spoke. He couldn't believe he was standing face to face with the woman he'd refused to forget.

"Time flies, that's for sure. I'm sorry I wasn't there for your going away party, but you know how it is when duty calls."

"Yeah, I know all too well. I was a bit disappointed when I didn't see you at work on my last day, but I knew you were out in the field."

"How do you like the new job?"

"I'm adjusting. I have a good team. More responsibilities and far less travel, but it's cool. How are things going at *About Us*?"

Lina looked away for a brief moment. "I guess things are going fine, over there. I no longer work for *About Us*."

"Are you serious?" The shock Charles felt was evident in his tone. His forehead wrinkled, causing a small V between his eyebrows. "What happened? I thought you enjoyed your job. I can't believe you up and left."

"Who says I left?" Lina snapped back, sounding offended. My position was eliminated along with a few others. Let's just say there are several people that are not happy with you, especially since you said there wouldn't be any changes."

Charles cupped his face with his hands, before sliding them down and folding his arms. "This doesn't make sense. I relayed to you all the information I had been given. I don't understand why any position was eliminated."

"According to Jackson, there were budget cuts. I can't speak for the others who were downsized, but as for me, I was told the board decided to use freelance work only and therefore my position was no longer necessary. I was given the option to submit my work to the magazine on a freelance basis."

Lina's phone rang, interrupting her conversation with Charles.

"Is your stomach tore up that bad? What is taking you so long?" Cheri practically yelled into the phone.

"Really, Cheri?" Lina replied, hoping Charles, who was standing close enough to touch, hadn't heard Cheri's remarks. "I ran into Charles. I've been standing here talking to him."

"Your old boss, Charles Davenport? Seriously?"

"Yes, my old boss. Where are y'all? I'll come and meet you."

Cheri recited her and David's location and ended the call.

Charles hated to be referred to as Lina's old boss, even though that was his official position in her life. He wanted to be more. He couldn't believe he had been given this opportunity and he wasn't about to let it pass him by.

Lina turned to Charles apologetically. "I forgot my friends are waiting on me. It was good seeing you."

Disregarding his own friends standing nearby, he touched her shoulder. "Lina, wait. If you don't mind, I'll walk with you."

"Okay," Lina replied, sounding unsure of her answer. The two headed to the location Cheri had given her.

Charles was the first to revisit their conversation. He felt talking about work was a good way to get her to relax into further topics. "I can't believe Jackson had the nerve to tell you, you could do freelance work for the company while simultaneously eliminating your job."

"Yeah, that was a trip, but it's cool. All things work together for the good. My business has grown quite a bit, so to be honest I welcomed the relief. Losing the job at *About Us* freed me up to focus on building my own business, which is always best. It's nice being my own boss, which is a feeling I had forgotten when I accepted the position at *About Us* from you."

"Oh, so what you're saying is, I put you in bondage, huh?" Charles twisted his lips and raised an eyebrow at Lina.

She looked at his expression and burst into laughter. Tapping him on his muscular arm, she said, "You know that's not what I'm saying. I was very grateful for the job offer at the time. I guess I just outgrew it. I have no regrets, that's for sure."

"No regrets?" Charles asked, slowing his pace.

"Nope, none at all. I'm a firm believer, everything happens for a reason. Therefore, there's no need for regrets."

Cheri saw Lina and Charles approaching and waved

them over. Lina made brief introductions before being whisked away by Cheri. Charles and David remained in place, striking up a conversation of their own.

"Girl, his pictures did him no justice. The man is fine," Cheri whispered, being careful not to let David hear her ogling over another man. "How did you hook up with him? I thought you were going to the restroom."

"It was pure coincidence. Don't read any more into it, Cheri, because I know you. You'll have us labeled as a couple before the sun sets."

"All I'm going to say is you didn't see what I saw. The man was looking at you like you were Meagan Good or somebody. He couldn't be more obvious, even if you are clueless."

"Whatever, Cheri. The only one that's being obvious right now is you. Let's get back over there before we raise too many questions."

"Okay," Cheri replied, rolling her eyes. "We'll see how it all plays out."

The four spent the rest of the afternoon together eating and enjoying one another's company. David was glad to have a man hanging out with them. Charles was a welcomed distraction from the giddiness his girlfriend and her best friend exuded.

As the day drew to a close they headed to their vehicles. The day had been eventful and they were all worn out. Charles walked with them to David's vehicle. Fortunately, he had driven his own vehicle and met up with his friends at the festival, therefore he didn't have to find his friends before leaving. He hated for the day to come to an end.

Cheri and David climbed into the vehicle, leaving Charles and Lina standing outside for privacy.

"I enjoyed hanging out with you today, Lina. I think this is the first time we've had the pleasure without the burden of work looming over our heads."

"You're right, it is," Lina agreed.

"When can I see you again? I mean, this was cool, very cool, and I enjoyed every minute. If you would allow me, I would like to take you out on a real date sometime."

Lina hesitated. She liked Charles, but it was hard disconnecting him from their previous work relationship. "Charles, you were my boss. That's weird."

"I'm no longer in that position and neither are you. Please don't let our past obligations stop us from spending time together now."

Lina considered his words. Although the work relationship was the only thing she mentioned, she knew in her heart it was not the main reason she wasn't screaming the yes she desperately wanted to say. She looked over at the car and saw Cheri's face plastered to the window.

"Why not," Lina said, surrendering. After all, Charles had only asked her on a date. It wasn't like she was going to sleep with him. She was tired of letting her status dictate her life. She had overcome the crippling mental effects of the disease in every other area of her life. It was time she stopped it from hindering her dating life.

Charles could see the reservation in Lina's eyes. He couldn't believe his ears when she agreed to go out with him. A smile parted his lips and reflected in his eyes. "Cool. May I get your number?" When Charles left his position at *About Us* he turned his work cell phone containing Lina's phone number over to Jackson.

The two exchanged phone numbers before Charles opened the door for Lina to get in the car. She climbed in and relaxed against the seat. She was happy about her decision to go out with Charles and couldn't wait for his call.

Chapter Nine

Charles turned the water off in the shower and toweled off. He looked forward to his date with Lina. After seeing her at The Taste he called her later the same evening. To his delight, it was the first of many calls the two of them would share. They learned a lot about each other during their travels while working together, but their recent conversations had been uninhibited. Lina was easy to talk to and although he believed their attraction was mutual, she seemed to be keeping him in the friend zone.

Lina was the type of woman Charles felt he could spend the rest of his life with. He had the advantage of working with her for several years so it wasn't like meeting a stranger. While working together Lina was guarded when it came to her personal life. She kept things professional while allowing bits and pieces of her personality to shine through. Getting to know Lina the person as opposed to Lina the employee had been exciting.

Splashing on cologne, Charles got dressed and headed out the door. Lina's apartment was a thirty-minute drive from his house and he didn't want to be late. From their past conversations, Charles knew Lina enjoyed outdoor events. She also liked to do things she considered adventurous. He'd planned a trip for them to Six Flags Great America in Gurnee. The hour drive would give them quality time together without having a phone separating them.

Arriving at the address Lina had given him, Charles parked his car and made his way up the short flight of stairs to her apartment door. He pressed the doorbell and stood back. A small dog barked in response to the chime of the bell. Lina was at the door within seconds.

Charles struggled to keep his mouth from falling open. Standing before him was the most beautiful woman he thought he'd ever seen. The soft pink spaghetti strap romper Lina wore showed enough for him to see the toned definition of her arms and legs but covered enough that she didn't look sleazy. On her feet she wore pink and white Converse covered in iridescent crystals. The shoelaces had been replaced by satin ribbons.

"You look stunning," Charles said, staring at her as if she would disappear if he turned his head or even blinked.

"Thank you. You look nice as well. Would you mind coming in for a moment. Cheri is on her way over to get Sweetie. She's going to watch her while we go out. I've been meaning to give her a key, but I haven't gotten around to it." Lina stepped aside so Charles could enter the apartment. She admired his physique as he walked past her and into the living room. The gray polo shirt he wore was no match for his bulging muscles. The fabric of his dark denim jeans stretched long to accommodate his towering stature.

You can have a seat on the couch if you'd like. I just received a text from Cheri. She should be here in about five minutes. Can I offer you something to drink?"

"No, I'm fine thank you," Charles replied. "Who is this little fuzzy friend of yours?" Charles asked, petting the small chocolate brown canine that hopped up on the couch next to him.

Lina reached down and picked up the precious pup. "This is Sweetie, my baby."

"Sweetie? I don't think I've ever known a dog named Sweetie," Charles teased. "What breed is she?"

"She's a cockapoo. I call her Sweetie for short. Her full name is Sweet Tea. When I first saw her and that beautiful brown coat I was instantly in love. I picked her up and she loved all on me. I thought she was sweet. So naturally being from the south, I figured the perfect name for her would be Sweet Tea, thus the name Sweetie." Lina beamed with pride like she had made a profound statement.

Charles watched Lina dance around the living room with the small dog. He could no longer restrain his laughter. Both Lina and Sweetie turned and looked at him as if he was crashing their party.

"What?" Lina chided. "You must not like dogs or something."

"Oh no, that's not it at all. In fact, I grew up having pets. It's very clear you and Sweetie have a loving relationship. Hopefully, there will be room for one more in your lives."

Before Lina could utter a response, the doorbell rang. "That must be Cheri." Lina bounced over to the door still holding Sweetie in her arms. A quick glance through the peephole revealed her assessment was correct. Lina opened the door for her friend who entered with arms outstretched.

Cheri pulled Sweetie from Lina's arms and stepped further into the room. "Hello, Charles. It's nice to see you again."

Charles rose from his seat and extended his hand to Cheri. Cheri placed her hand inside of his, accepting the handshake.

Cheri sat down on the sofa and placed Sweetie on the floor, allowing her to roam free. "What do you guys have planned for today?" Cheri asked.

"I'm taking Lina to Great America," Charles answered.

"I sure hope you're prepared because Lina loves to get on all the thrill rides." Cheri continued pointing at the pants Charles was wearing. "I hope you don't get too hot standing in the long lines with those jeans on."

"We'll be fine. I purchased the Flash Pass for each of us. I'm sure our wait will be minimal," Charles replied.

Lina looked over at her friend and raised an eyebrow. Cheri returned the gesture. "Don't let me hold you any longer. The drive to Gurnee is no joke," Cheri said, making herself comfortable on the couch. She picked up the remote and pressed the power button. "You two have fun. Me and Sweetie are going to watch some movies and chill."

Charles stepped over to the door and opened it for Lina. She walked through calling out to Cheri to come and lock the door.

"Thank you for agreeing to this," Charles said, looking over at Lina. "I haven't been to Great America in years. I'm looking forward to seeing all the new attractions."

"I try to go at least once a year. I have loved roller coasters since I was young. Besides, walking the huge park is great exercise."

"We've got a long ride ahead of us. How do you feel about grabbing a bite to eat before we hit the expressway?"

"That sounds like a plan. At least our food will have time to digest. There's nothing worse than getting on a ride with a full stomach. I want something light though; a sandwich or salad would be great."

"I agree." Charles maneuvered his car down the busy city street. He pulled into the parking lot for Subway. Securing a spot near the entrance, he turned off the ignition and walked around the car to open the door for Lina. As he approached, the door swung open, barely missing him.

"Oh, I'm sorry," Lina said, holding her hand up in surrender. "I'm used to jumping out of the car when I get where I'm going. I didn't hit you, did I?"

"No, I'm good." He laughed. "I won't lie, you almost took a brotha out. I need you to get used to me opening doors for you."

"I guess I'm out of practice. Thank you though." Lina stepped out of the car and moved aside for Charles to push the door closed. She didn't know why she was suddenly becoming nervous around him. They had worked together for years. When they traveled on assignments Charles always opened doors for her. The reality of being on an actual date with a man she silently had crushed on for so long was starting to kick in.

Lina had often fantasized about dating Charles. Only Cheri knew her true feelings for her then boss. They spent countless hours together hanging out, traveling, and sharing meals. Lina felt safe knowing she could use their working relationship as a wall to hide behind. She would never jeopardize her employment for the sake of passing feelings, but now the tables had turned. She and Charles were free to date and explore a relationship if it developed into that. The thought of it all left her feeling vulnerable.

The couple walked inside the restaurant and ordered their meals. Charles opted for a grilled chicken sandwich with all the trimmings. Lina chose to go with a salad, loaded with veggies. Once they received their order, they sat down in a booth with a view overlooking the busy street.

"It almost looks funny seeing you out without a camera," Charles said to Lina before taking a bite of his sandwich.

"Photography is not all I do in my life, Charles," Lina replied while stabbing the salad with her fork. She placed the leafy mixture into her mouth and chewed before continuing. Although she would never admit it, she didn't care much for carrying on a conversation during a meal. However, she would indulge him. If the relationship progressed at any point, he would get to know her and reserve his conversations once the meal started.

Charles nodded as if there was a tune playing only he could hear. He noticed Lina hadn't expounded on her response, but instead started to eat. He figured, she must have been hungry. Charles decided to allow her to eat a bit more before continuing the conversation, distracting himself with his own meal.

They continued their meals engaging in light banter that required brief responses. Lina pushed aside her salad and took a few sips of water. Charles balled up the wrapper from his sandwich and collected their trash from the table.

"I'm going to run to the ladies' room real quick before we head out. I'll be back in just a second." Lina slid out of the booth and headed in the direction of the sign posted at the back of the restaurant.

Charles took the trash and placed it in the bin. Following Lina's lead, he headed to the men's room. He came out and found Lina standing in the restaurant near the exit. He joined her and pushed the door open for her. Removing the keys from his pocket, he pressed the unlock button on the key fob and followed Lina around to the passenger side.

"You are such a gentleman, Charles, but you don't have to open my door every time. I promise I won't deduct points from you."

"I don't mind at all. This is who I am, Lina. It's not an act or my way of trying to gain points. I had the privilege of watching my father treat my mother like a queen. I saw how it made my mother feel, and I knew it was a pattern for me to follow." He pulled the door open and allowed her to slide in. Closing the door, he stepped around to the driver's door and joined her inside. Charles pressed his foot on the brake pedal and pushed the ignition button causing the engine to roar.

"Are your parents still together?" Lina asked, shyly. Up until that point, they hadn't discussed their families. Their previous conversations had been basic and free from probing questions.

"Yes, they're still together, which I know is a blessing. Our family was one of very few on our block that had both parents in the home. Some of my buddies had stepparents for various reasons, but most of them were raised by single mothers."

"Where did you grow up?"

"Right here, baby. Chi town's finest. I was born and raised on the South side."

"Oh, so you're a native," Lina said sarcastically. "Would you ever consider leaving? I mean, things are getting pretty rough here. Most of the people I know are choosing to relocate."

Charles maneuvered his car onto Interstate 94. "I can't say I won't, but to be honest, I also can't say I will. I've never had to make the choice."

"I like Chicago. Moving here has been a great

experience. Being the youngest child, it wasn't easy gaining my independence at home in Durham. Since I moved to Chicago, which is definitely not right around the corner from my parents, I've had the opportunity to grow up and find out who I am outside of my position in the family. This constant rising crime rate isn't helping things much. Being a single woman, away from all my family, wears on me at times."

"I won't lie, I love my city and all the good it offers, but I don't think I would want to raise a family here."

Lina pressed her back into the soft leather seat, it was something she did when she was nervous or upset. The curve of the seat reminded her of a gentle hug. An instant feeling of discomfort threatened to consume her. Although she had heard stories of people who were HIV positive giving birth to children that didn't carry the virus, it was a risk she wasn't willing to take. Knowing she had passed the virus on to anyone, especially a child, would be devastating.

Charles noticed the change in Lina's demeanor. He considered prying but realized it wasn't the best idea with this being their first real date. There were so many questions going through his mind. Did Lina want children, better yet did she even like children? He thought about her bond with her dog, Sweetie. She was extremely affectionate with the pup. He felt like he had been kicked in the gut when he considered she may not be able to have children, which would have made his remark about raising a family seem insensitive.

He knew he was putting far too much thought into the subject, but he couldn't help it. Charles was tired of casual dating and the uncertainty that went along with it.

He wanted someone he could call his own, a woman who would accept him despite his troubled past. He needed a woman who desired him and not his financial portfolio.

The lack of conversation allowed the soulful sounds on the radio to fill the space. One by one, old school rhythm and blues songs played through the speakers, causing both Charles and Lina to bob to the beat. When the song *Nobody's Supposed to Be Here* by Deborah Cox came on, Lina could no longer resist. She closed her eyes and sang her heart out. Snapping her fingers between hand and arm gestures, she bellowed with passion.

Charles glanced over at her and raised his cheek in a half smile. He inwardly wished she was singing the song to him. When she nailed the high note, he no longer remained silent. "Wow, you better sing, girl."

She was so enthralled in the song she dismissed him with a wave of her hand and continued her impromptu concert.

Once the song ended, Charles teased her. "That must be your jam, huh?"

"Yes, it is," Lina replied and poked her lips out in defiance, garnering laughs from both she and Charles. "I love that song. I used to play it all the time. Man, I haven't heard it in so long. I'm gonna have to download it to my phone."

Charles put on his turn signal and shifted his vehicle to the right, taking the exit for Illinois 132 East. "You have a banging voice. I'll have to take you to a karaoke bar so you can showcase your talent. Have you ever sung professionally?"

"Just simple stuff, like school talent shows and church. Me, my sister, Javonne, and my cousin, Erin, use to think we were the stuff. We would win just about every talent show we entered. My other sister, Zarion, was too busy with sports to care anything about singing."

"What happened to the group?" Charles was intrigued.

"Nothing. We were in Durham. There weren't any big time music producers looking for us in Durham. First my sister graduated, leaving me and Erin. We tried to continue as a duo, but it wasn't the same. Eventually we found other hobbies. I think that's when I got more involved in photography."

"You could still make it as a singer if you wanted to. You're good, and I'm not just saying it to make you feel good. I'm serious."

"Thank you for the compliment, but I'll pass. My true passion is photography. I feel blessed to be able to do what I love for a living." Lina's eyes widened as signs for the theme park came into view. She felt like a kid whenever she came to Great America. She felt free to enjoy the moment without having to focus on the realities of her life.

Charles paid the parking attendant and perused the massive parking lot for an available slot. He was glad Lina had loosened up. His objective for the day was for her to enjoy herself. He didn't want anything to interfere with that. Charles found a parking spot and carefully parked his vehicle."

Once they exited the vehicle, Lina grabbed Charles by the hand and pulled him toward the entrance. "Let's get this party started!"

Chapter Ten

"Girl, you have worn me out." Charles pulled Lina over to an awaiting bench and took a seat. "I thought I was in better shape, but you have proven otherwise."

Lina sat down next to him and shook her head. "Can't hang, huh?" she teased. "We haven't even covered half the park. You can't give up already."

"I'm not giving up, believe that. I'm just chilling for a minute. I can admit, when you said you love this place, you weren't exaggerating."

"What's not to love? Any place that will bring joy to this many people at one time is nothing short of amazing."

"You may have a point there," Charles agreed. "Most of the people here do look happy."

"Happiness is happiness even if it's only temporary. We all have enough troubles in this life. I try to latch on to happiness whenever I can."

Charles lowered his voice and looked deep into Lina's eyes. "Do you want to know what would make me happy?"

Lina was taken aback. Up until this point Charles had been cool and hadn't approached her in a sexual way. She didn't know how to react. "What's that?" she asked, just above a whisper.

He spoke slow and seductively, "Food."

"What!" Lina exclaimed before bursting into laughter.

"Yeah, I'm hungry." Charles looked at her and squinted.

"What did you think I was going to say?"

"Nothing. You're a mess, Charles." Lina continued to laugh. "We can get something to eat, but let's make it something light. We still have to get on the American Eagle, and I know you don't want to ride that roller coaster on a full stomach."

"Agreed." Charles stood from the bench and took Lina by the hand, helping her up. "The County Fair Food Court is over there, he said, pointing to his right. I'm pretty sure I can get a burger and fries at one of those stands."

"Sounds like a plan," Lina agreed.

The couple walked hand in hand to the food court. For Lina, being with Charles felt natural. Having worked together for so long she felt she knew him. He had a great sense of humor, which she adored, and had always been respectful of her. Lina wished her life and health was different. Why couldn't she be normal? Knowing one poor decision had completely altered her life, robbing her of the potential love she knew she deserved and a family she would never have, caused her to weep inside. She eased her hand out of Charles' grip. When he looked down at her she offered him a playful smile to distract him.

"Ooh look, Charles, they have corn dogs over there," she stated, pointing to one of the stands in the food court. "I'd rather have a corn dog instead of a burger."

"No problem, we can get corn dogs instead." Charles started walking in the direction Lina pointed.

Lina grabbed his arm and pulled him back. "Wait, where are you going?"

"You said you wanted corn dogs so I'm going to get corn dogs." Charles looked confused.

"*I* want a corn dog. That doesn't mean you can't still get

a burger." Lina pointed at the stand offering burgers. "You get in line for your burger and I'll go over there and get the corn dog. I'm a big girl, I can handle it."

Charles reached into his pocket and pulled out some cash. He extended the folded bills to Lina.

She held up her hand in protest. "That's okay, I got it." Before Charles could offer a rebuttal, she skipped off to the corn dog stand.

They purchased their meals and took a seat at a nearby table. Lina pressed the corner of a mustard package, giving herself room to tear the corner off without spilling the contents on her hands and clothes. Squeezing the packet, she distributed the yellow substance throughout the length of the fried breaded frank. She took a bite from the side of her corn dog and moaned in delight.

Charles filled his mouth with a bite of his double cheeseburger and a few fries chasing them down with three large gulps of Coke. He enjoyed watching the way Lina rocked from side to side, tapping her heel as she ate. Over the years he had observed her healthy appetite. Whatever she wanted to eat she ate, whether they were traveling for work, or having a meal along with the rest of the team in the office. He often wondered how she had maintained a slender figure. He guessed she either worked out a lot or had a fast metabolism.

Lina took a sip of water and shifted her attention from her meal to a set of teenage twins. She wondered how anyone could tell them apart due to their uncanny resemblance. "Do you have any siblings?" she asked Charles, turning her attention back to him.

"Yeah, I have a younger sister," he answered. "What about you? I know you have at least two sisters. You mentioned them earlier."

"We'll get to me in a minute. Right now, I want to know about you. Tell me about your sister."

"There isn't much to tell. She's five years younger than me. I was always protective of her growing up, but she felt I was overprotective. Since she was the baby, my parents would tend to let her get away with far too much. As a result, she's made some poor choices."

"Are the two of you close?"

"I believe so. We're close enough to keep in contact, but not so close we can't lead our own lives."

"I understand," Lina said, nodding. "Shoot, I can even sympathize with her in regard to being the youngest. I'm the youngest of four, two sisters and a brother. My siblings were always on my case. They are one of the main reasons I moved from Durham. My parents are already overprotective and they're worse than my mom and dad." Lina dipped some fries into a small cup of ketchup and popped them in her mouth.

"Which one am I going to have to watch out for the most?" Charles asked.

Tilting her head, Lina tried to read his expression. Giving him the benefit of the doubt, she answered, "There is not one in particular. Every single one of them will put you through the ringer."

"That's alright, I can handle it," Charles replied with a wink.

"How about we handle the American Eagle?" Lina gathered up their trash and dumped it in a nearby bin.

Charles stood up and joined Lina. He grabbed her hand. "Fine, if the American Eagle is what you want, the American Eagle you shall get. Let's go." He kissed her on the cheek and escorted her to the roller coaster. Noticing the tight-lipped smile Lina displayed, Charles was determined to not be deterred. He wanted to be more than Lina's former employer, he wanted to be her man. It was time for him to get out of the friend zone.

Chapter Eleven

"Tell me everything and don't leave nothing out." Cheri sat on the couch with her feet tucked under her legs. She gently petted Sweetie who was resting comfortably in her lap.

The phone rang, drawing Lina and Cheri's attention before Lina could speak. Lina picked up the phone and viewed the display.

"Is that him?" Cheri asked, trying to look at the phone.

"No, it's Zarion." Lina turned the phone so Cheri could see the image of her nephew on the screen.

"Put her on speaker so we can talk together."

Lina rolled her eyes but complied with her friend's request. "Hold on, Z, I'm putting you on speaker." Lina pressed the button and held the phone in her hand so she and Cheri could both hear the conversation.

"What's going on?" Lina asked her sister.

"Not much, I'm just chilling. Daniel is finally asleep so I can get some me time. Anyway, you know good and well I didn't call to talk about me. Tell me about your date."

"Exactly, stop stalling, Lina." Cheri chimed in.

"Y'all, it was amazing," Lina squealed. "We had so much fun. I tried to get on every ride, but Charles couldn't hang. He pretended like he wasn't fazed, but the look on his face when we were on the American Eagle gave him away. That man was terrified." The ladies laughed in unison.

"It always trips me out when I see grown men get scared on a rollercoaster. I be looking at them like, really dude," Cheri said.

"Don't be so hard on the brother. Not everybody is into thrill rides. Knowing you, you're not telling the whole story. I'll bet it wasn't the first ride you took him on. With the way you act at amusement parks y'all were probably about six rides in by the time you got on the American Eagle."

"Your assessment may or may not be true. I shall neither confirm nor deny."

Laughing, Zarion replied, "Why am I not surprised?"

"Forget you, Z." Lina pushed Cheri's shoulder. "And you too, Cheri."

"I know you had to do more than ride a roller coaster, otherwise this super fun date you're talking about sounds quite boring," Cheri said.

"Of course, we did more than ride roller coasters. We spent the whole day together. We had great conversations and I swear when he held my hand I felt electricity go throughout my body."

"Not electricity," Zarion mocked, garnering another round of laughter from the group.

"I'm serious y'all. I really like him, and to be honest it scares me. First of all, it's weird. This guy used to be my boss. Even though we don't work together anymore, dating him still seems inappropriate."

Cheri jumped in. "He's not your boss anymore, so all bets are off. Plus, you have been crazy about the man for the longest. I think it's pretty cool he seems to be into you as much as you are him. Lina, you have every right to be happy like everyone else in the world. Tell her, Z."

"She's right, baby sis. I say, if you like him and he seems

to like you too, then go for it. You don't know what may come out of this."

Lina placed her phone on the table, jumped up from the couch, and paced in front of the coffee table. "You two make it sound so easy, talking about go for it, you like him, he likes you. I would love to go for it, but y'all are trying to act like everything with me is normal. I'm not like you Cheri, or you Zarion. I can't just go for it. Besides," Lina plopped back down on the couch and took Sweetie from Cheri. "None of this will matter once he finds out I'm HIV positive. Like it or not, he is going to run as far from me as he can get."

"Why do you always have to bring your illness up?" Zarion asked, her tone filled with sarcasm. "Truth be told I think you're hiding behind your status to keep men at bay."

"How could you say that, Z? You have no idea what it's like living with this disease."

"Yeah, I know, we've heard it all before. The reality is, there are people, both men and women, who live with the disease every day who have found and kept love. It's not the death sentence it used to be. If you want to find and keep love, you can. Like Mama and Daddy always taught us from the Bible to call the things that are not as if they were. You can either speak love in your life or loneliness. The choice is up to you. I believe that to be true and you can't change my mind."

"You don't get it, but that's cool. You don't have to because it's not your life. The truth is I like Charles a lot. A whole lot as a matter of fact, and the reality of him rejecting me the way Maxwell did all because of my status would be unbearable."

Cheri scooted closer to Lina on the couch and placed her

arm around Lina's shoulder. "It's okay, bestie. Remember Charles is not Maxwell and if you two are meant to be together, you will be, regardless of your status. I see both you and your sister's point, but I have to agree with Zarion on this one. You can't give up based on what you think will happen. Give Charles the benefit of the doubt. If it doesn't work out, it's because it's not meant."

"I'm going to tell him," Lina blurted.

"What?" Zarion yelled into the phone, causing Sweetie to lift her head and look in the direction of the device. "Why would you tell him, especially this soon? Maybe you should get to know him better before you jump off the deep end and reveal something so personal. You've only had one date with the man, and it was at an amusement park. How about you go on a real date, matter of fact, go on a few dates, and then make the decision about telling him. Right now, it's too soon."

"Nope, I disagree," Lina said. "I think now is the best time. I've known him for years so it's not like he's a guy I met out of the blue. The more time I spend with him, the more attached I could become, which would make delaying the inevitable a huge mistake. I may as well rip the bandage off and see what happens." Lina snuggled Sweetie close to her heart and rubbed her wavy brown fur. "If it doesn't work out with Charles at least I know my baby is still going to love me." The puppy rewarded her by licking her cheek.

"It doesn't matter what we say because one thing is for sure, you're going to do whatever you want to do anyway." Zarion's frustration with her sister was evident in her tone. "I won't even waste my breath trying to convince you otherwise. I'm glad you had fun and I hope he really is the man for you. If he is, he'll do right by you. Now, I need to get off this phone and get some rest. Your nephew will be awake before the birds and God knows I need my rest. I love you, baby sis. It was good talking to you too, Cheri."

Lina and Cheri said their goodbyes to Zarion and Cheri pressed the button to end the call. Cheri rose from the couch and headed in the direction of the kitchen.

"I'm thirsty. Do you want anything to drink while I'm going?" she asked Lina.

"Yeah, I'll take a glass of tea if there's any left."

Cheri retrieved two glasses from the cabinet and filled them with ice. She poured tea into Lina's glass before filling her glass with fruit punch. Cheri turned her glass up and took a few sips. Returning to the living room she placed her glass on the table and handed Lina the glass of tea.

"Are you really going to tell Charles about your status this soon? Maybe your sister has a point. This is pretty early."

"I hope you're not going to start on this again. Like I told Zarion, Charles is not a new guy. We've known each other for years. It's better to tell him now before any real feelings get involved than to wait around. I know he's not Maxwell, but I can't take a chance of having a repeat of how Maxwell did me. That was too much. I don't ever want to go through anything like that again."

"Okay," Cheri picked up her glass and took another sip. "How are you going to do it? Better yet, when are you going to do it? Will you at least wait until your next date?"

"I'm going to let things flow. I don't really want to tell him over the phone but that may not be a bad idea."

"Girl, you can't tell him something like that over the phone. Are you crazy? Those rollercoasters must have flipped you on your head one time too many."

Defeated, Lina sat Sweetie on the couch next to her and turned to Cheri. "How am I supposed to know how to tell him? I've never done this before. The only people I have really had to tell were my family and my doctors. Maxwell found out when he saw my meds in the bathroom, and you, you're my best friend. It was difficult telling you, but I'm not in a physical relationship with you."

Cheri didn't know how to fix things for her friend. She couldn't imagine what life was like for Lina. She refused to pretend like she did. She could sympathize but her sympathy would only go so far.

"When everything is said and done you have to make the best choice for you, Lina. You're right about what you said earlier. Although your sister and I both love you dearly we don't live your life and we can't make this decision for you. If Charles is meant to be in your life, he'll stick around. If he's not, then he won't. Either way, God has a man for you who will love you unconditionally."

Cheri looked down at her watch and noted the time. "It's getting late. You've had a long day so I'm sure you're exhausted. I'm pretty tired myself so I'm going to head home." Cheri hugged Lina and rose from the couch. "I'm glad you're getting out and allowing yourself to feel again, bestie. That's a good sign."

Lina stood up and joined her. They walked to the front door together. "Be safe going home, Cheri. Make sure you call me and let me know when you make it."

"I will. Keep me posted on the Charles situation."

Once Cheri was secure in her car and pulling away, Lina closed and locked her door. Sweetie was on her heels, matching every step. She kneeled down and patted the pooch on top of her head. "Time for bed, Sweetie." With well-trained steps, Sweetie climbed into her pet bed and curled into a ball, resting her head on the edge of the bed.

Pulling open the top drawer of the mahogany chest of drawers located near her bedroom window, Lina reached in and pulled out her favorite nightgown. She looked at the rhinestone-studded gown and traced the words *I believe in miracles* with her index finger. The saying was true. Despite her current situation, she did believe in miracles. If her life was going to change, it was going to take a miracle.

Lina walked into the bathroom and turned on the shower. She shed her garments and stuck her hand into the spray of water, testing the temperature. Satisfied, she stepped inside and allowed the massaging pulse of water to sooth her aching muscles. Closing her eyes, she inhaled a full breath, filling her lungs. As the air expelled in a slow continuous rhythm, Lina's mind drifted to Charles. Dating him had been a quiet fantasy she'd held for years. Having a crush on him was easy because she never felt anything would come of it given their work relationship.

Warm water beat against Lina's skin, placing her in a state of tranquility. It was in moments such as this when she felt a closer bond with the Lord. Lina imagined her problems being transported away from her like discarded water rushing through the drain. As thoughts of Charles invaded her mind, Lina struggled to keep her attention focused on the task at hand. She rubbed lavender scented body wash on her skin and massaged it in.

In silence, she offered up thanks and presented her petitions to the Lord. *Dear God, thank you for all the blessings you've given me. I love you and I honor you. Father, you know my beginning and my end. I come now seeking guidance concerning Charles. I don't want my heart to be broken. If it's your will for me to inform him of my condition, and to continue seeing him I ask you to give me peace in my heart and mind. I know you have wonderful things in store for me. Please keep me on the right path. In Jesus name I pray, Amen.*

Lina placed her hand on the handle and turned it until it stopped in the off position. Grabbing a plush towel from the bar attached to the outside of the shower door, she dried off and wrapped her body in the warm soft fabric. Her phone buzzed, indicating an incoming call. Lina rushed into her bedroom to answer the call before it switched over to voicemail. The ringing stopped and her phone displayed a notification indicating she had missed a call from Cheri.

Before Lina could dial Cheri's number back, her phone buzzed again. She wasn't surprised because Cheri rarely let a missed call go unnoticed without repeating the call. Lina slid her nightgown over her head and sat on the edge of the bed. Pressing the answer button, a smile formed on her lips.

"I didn't wake you, did I?" Charles' sexy, baritone voice flowed through the phone's speaker.

"No, I'm not in bed yet. What's going on?"

"I enjoyed being with you today. That's the most fun I've had in a while. I almost felt like a kid, jumping on all of those rides, and filling up on carnival foods. I had almost forgotten about funnel cakes until today."

Lina chuckled. "I had a great time as well. Thank you for taking me."

"The pleasure was all mine. I know this is short notice, but I can't wait to see you again. What are you doing tomorrow?"

Chapter Twelve

"When you said you wanted to see me again this is not at all what I expected," Lina said to Charles. She looked up at the large brick structure.

"It'll be okay. Trust me on this." Charles extended his arm to Lina and encouraged her to place her arm through the open space. Once she complied, he placed his free hand on top of hers and escorted her inside the building. Music blared from the speakers, welcoming them.

"Good morning, Charles," a jolly man greeted once they were inside. "Who is this lovely lady you have on your arm?"

"Hey, Eddie. This is Lina."

Ignoring her extended hand, Eddie offered a wide grin and pulled Lina into his arms, practically knocking her back with his girth. "We do hugs around here." He released her and Lina stumbled back. "It's good to have you. Charles here is a good man, hopefully we'll get to see more of you."

Lina smiled but didn't answer. She had yet to talk to Charles and, therefore, refused to make a promise she wasn't sure she would be able to keep.

Taking Lina by the hand, Charles pulled her away. "Alright, Eddie. It was good talking to you. We better get inside. I'll talk to you later."

With a few short steps Charles and Lina entered the

sanctuary. They were greeted by an usher giving the couple a warm smile and donation envelopes. Lina continued in step with Charles until they arrived at a section located to the right of the stage. He stepped aside and allowed her to take a seat before sitting next to her.

Lina sat with her back against the chair and admired the glamour of the sanctuary. Thick eggplant colored chairs were used in the place of pews. Large crystal chandeliers with gold trimming hung throughout the massive space. The stage stood three feet above the floor. The choir stand was behind and to the left of a large glass podium. The band area was on the other side of the stage on the right.

A man appearing to be in his early twenties took to the stage with three women and two men backing him up. "Everybody get on your feet and praise the Lord." He raised and lowered his hand, pumping the crowd up.

With flawless unison the praise team swayed to the music as they lifted their voices in song. Charles and Lina were on their feet clapping and singing along with the other parishioners. Lina had been reserved when Charles first invited her to church. The invitation had come as a surprise. After spending a fun filled day at the amusement park, Lina thought Charles was calling to say goodnight. Instead he'd asked her to join him for church.

The music died down and Lina and Charles took their seats. Charles leaned over to Lina and pointed to a slender man seated in the pulpit that towered over the other men sitting around him. "That's our pastor—Theodore Youngblood."

"His name certainly fits. How old is he anyway? He doesn't look a day over eighteen," Lina said with a raised eyebrow.

"I'm not sure how old he is but I know he's at least twenty-five."

Lina nodded her understanding. "Who's the frumpy guy sitting next to him?" she asked, focusing on the man sitting to Pastor Youngblood's right. His pecan complexion was filled with blemishes. A fat pocket sitting on the back of his egg shaped, bald head, resembled a hotdog. Despite his undesirable appearance, he wore a tailored black suit with a maroon shirt and diamond encrusted cufflinks.

Charles shrugged. "I've never seen him before. He must be the guest speaker."

Pastor Youngblood rose from his seat and approached the podium. "God is good," he called out.

"All the time," the congregation replied in unison.

"And all the time," Pastor Youngblood continued.

"God is good," the congregation called back.

"People of God, it's a blessing to be in the house of the Lord one more time. I don't know about you, but I woke up blessed. When my eyes opened this morning, a smile formed on my lips and I declared this is the day the Lord has made, so I'm going to rejoice and be glad. Does anybody feel like rejoicing with me?"

The musicians followed the pastor's request with a high tempo beat. Members of the congregation clapped their hands and rose from their seat. Pastor Youngblood tapped his feet and raised his shoulders in a dance that resembled a sanctified club dance. After several minutes, Pastor Youngblood raised his hands, encouraging the congregants to take a seat. The organist switched to a slower melodic tune.

"Ain't no harm in praising the Lord," Pastor Youngblood said with raised hands. He allowed the congregation time to settle down before continuing. "Family, we're in for a treat today. You all know, I won't put anyone up before you who isn't living the Word they preach. I've known this man for several years and he has always shown himself to be a true man of God. The hour is far spent, so without any further ado I present to you my friend, Elder Jasper Clayton."

Elder Clayton rose and embraced Pastor Youngblood. The congregation welcomed him with applause.

"Thank you all so much. It is truly an honor to be here with you today. Pastor Youngblood and I go way back so it was with great honor that I accepted his invitation today. Before I get started I would like to acknowledge my beautiful fiancée, Sister Maxine. Stand up, sweetheart and greet the people.

Lina's breath caught in her throat as she watched Maxine Miller stand and wave at the crowd like she had just won the Miss America pageant. She couldn't believe her eyes. Standing before her was the same woman who went out of her way to gain Maxwell's attention. Seeing as though Maxwell was now married, Lina wasn't surprised Maxine had moved on to another man. The fitted knee length dress Maxine wore hugged every curve she had. The color matched Elder Clayton's shirt. A diamond broach sat in the center of her dress. Topping off her outfit was a maroon and black wide brim hat and matching pumps.

Looking at the couple, Lina rolled her eyes. Judging by Elder Clayton's and Maxine's appearance. Lina couldn't imagine a more mix matched couple. "Humph, opportunist," Lina spat barely above a whisper.

Charles turned to Lina and eyed her suspiciously. "Did you say something?"

"No, it's nothing." Lina patted him on the back of his hand, hoping to distract him.

"Do you know her?" Charles asked, not willing to let the subject go.

"Not exactly. I've seen her a time or two."

"Oh okay," Charles replied, dropping the subject.

Elder Clayton made a few more acknowledgments before beginning his sermon. He delivered a powerful message about persevering in the face of defeat. He encouraged the congregation to expect good in their lives despite their current situation. Using himself as an example, he shared a testimony of how he had allowed life's situations to bring him to the point of giving up. He told them it was in his darkest hour when he felt the hand of God holding him and encouraging him to live. It was at that moment when his life began to change for the better.

Lina took note of his words and held them in her heart. She no longer focused on Maxine. Instead she chose to apply the words Elder Clayton had spoken to her own life. No matter what the result, she felt peace about her decision to share her status with Charles. She took his hand into hers and squeezed gently. Lina wanted to savor the moment because she knew it could very well be the last time she would be this close to him. She leaned over and whispered in his ear, "Remind me to tell you something when we leave here."

Chapter Thirteen

The church service concluded and the congregants made their way into the aisles, shuffling toward the exit doors. Lina glanced over her shoulder and noticed Maxine ogling over Elder Clayton. Charles took her by the hand and escorted her toward the exit doors.

"I don't know about you, but I'm starved," Charles stated, opening the door for Lina to get inside his vehicle. He closed the door and quickly moved to the driver's side.

Lina waited until Charles was secure inside before responding. She wasn't sure how she'd be able to eat with the huge knot that had formed in her belly. She knew before the day ended she would be disclosing everything to him. Lina hoped Charles would respond in a positive manner, but she understood his reaction was beyond her control.

Noticing her silence, Charles turned to her. "Do you have the taste for anything in particular?" he asked.

"Not really. Wherever you decide to go I'm sure I'll find something I like."

"That works." Charles pulled out of the parking lot and turned left. He drove a short distance before turning in to Red Lobster. He pulled into a slot near the entrance and moved his gearshift to the Park position. Looking over at Lina, he smiled before lifting her left hand to his lips and planting a soft kiss. "I hope you don't mind seafood. I'm in the mood for surf and turf."

"Seafood will work. See, I knew you'd make the right decision," Lina said rewarding Charles with a smile of her own. *Hopefully he'll make the right decision concerning us,* she thought. Lina sat patiently and waited for Charles to open her door.

"Let's go, sweetheart," he said, taking her hand and lifting her out of the car.

"Careful now, a girl could get used to this."

"As you should."

The couple entered the restaurant and were seated immediately. The hostess placed a menu in front of each of them and stepped away from the table.

"I guess we beat the lunch crowd," Charles said, scanning the near empty dining room. "At least I hope that's the case. An empty restaurant is not usually a good sign."

"I'm sure it's fine. We got out of church pretty early. This place will probably be full before we can get our meals."

A server approached them, smiling. She wore a white button-down shirt with black slacks and a short black apron filled with straws. Placing a basket of biscuits on the table she took a step back and greeted the couple. "Good afternoon. My name is Kristen. What can I get you guys to drink?"

"I'll have water with lemon on the side," Lina said, returning the server's smile.

Turning her attention to Charles, Kristen asked, "And for you, sir?"

"I'll take a Coke."

"Okay, I'll get your drinks while you look over the menu.

"Hey, let me ask you a quick question," Charles said,

preventing Kristen from leaving.

"Of course, how can I help you, sir?"

"Is this restaurant always this empty? I don't think I've ever seen a Red Lobster this empty."

Kristen stifled a laugh. "I'm not sure what the case is right now, but typically we're pretty busy. I'm sure it'll pick up once people start getting out and about and when churches start dismissing."

"Good. I was about to say, I don't want to be up in here if this restaurant failed inspection or something."

The server's fair skin turned crimson. "No, sir. We always maintain an A rating. You're in good hands. I'll be right back with your drinks." She giggled as she stepped away.

Lina reached over and slapped Charles on the back of the hand. "I can't believe you said that. The poor girl didn't know how to respond." Lina couldn't help but laugh.

Charles shrugged. "It's like this, I could either sit here and wonder, or I could ask. I chose to ask."

"Do you feel better now that you've asked?"

"Nope. I'll feel better when I see some more people walk through those doors," he stated, pointing at the large wood double doors." He picked up a biscuit and inspected it before peeling off a piece and putting it in his mouth.

"I don't know what I'm going to do with you. You're a trip." Lina shook her head and continued to laugh. She wasn't surprised by his actions in the least. She had seen Charles do similar things throughout the years when they went on work related outings.

Kristen returned to take their order. "See, sir, I told you there was no need to worry. There are more people coming in right now." Smiling, she looked in the direction of a large crowd entering the restaurant.

"Yeah, right. I bet you went in the back and called them people. That's what took you so long, isn't it?" The trio burst into laughter.

"You know what, thank you, sir. I haven't had this much fun at work in a long time. I needed a good laugh today." Continuing to smile, she asked, "Are you all ready to order?"

Charles bowed his head in Lina's direction prompting her to order first. "I'd like the Shrimp Linguini Alfredo and you can give him the Rock Lobster and steak. Please cook the steak medium well."

"I'll get this order in right away." Kristen removed the menus and stepped away from the table.

Raising his eyebrow, Charles gave Lina a sidelong glance. "How do you know I wanted to order the Rock Lobster and steak?"

"Because you said you had the taste for surf and turf when we were in the car. Plus, you always ordered the same thing every time we went to Red Lobster when we worked together."

"So, you've been paying attention, I see."

"I pay attention to everything. I'm a single woman living in Chicago. My life could depend on it. Just like I was paying attention today at church. I enjoyed the service a lot. I'm embarrassed to say I haven't attended church in a while." Lina brought up church to steer Charles from the direction she saw the conversation going. She wasn't ready to talk about them.

"I knew you would like it. I've been attending there for a little over a year. The man you met when we first arrived..."

"Eddie?"

"Yeah, good ole Eddie. He's the one that introduced me

to the church. He lives in my parents' neighborhood. I've known him since I was a kid."

"Has he always been so jolly and so...round?"

"Aw, man, Lina. Don't do my man like that. You may not believe it, but Eddie was very athletic when he was younger. He had a promising career in football until he tore his ACL."

Lina dropped her eyes. She knew she was wrong for judging Eddie so harshly. When she saw him her immediate thought was how could he let himself get so out of shape. She figured, of all people, she should have been the last to judge.

Kristen returned with their meals and placed them on the table. Lina was grateful for the distraction. Once the server left the table they bowed their heads and Charles blessed the food.

"I've been looking forward to this," he declared, slicing off a piece of steak. He added a bite of potatoes to the end of his fork and placed the combo in his mouth. He nodded as he chewed. "Ummm, it's perfect. Just the way I like it."

Although Charles was referring to his meal, a pain of disappointment shot through Lina's body, causing her belly to fill with butterflies. She considered perhaps she was being overly sensitive but the fear of rejection was threatening to overtake her. She used her fork and pushed the food around on her plate.

"Is something wrong with your meal?" Charles asked before shoving a forkful of lobster into his mouth.

"No, it's fine. I'm feeling a little queasy. I'm sure it'll pass." Lina looked over at his plate and saw he was halfway finished with his meal. "I see you were hungry."

"Yeah, I was running a little late this morning so I

skipped breakfast." Charles placed his fork on the edge of the plate. "If you're not feeling well I can have the server wrap our meals to go and I'll take you home."

"No please, go ahead and eat. I'm fine. It's already starting to pass, see." Lina twirled her fork in the noodles and placed the bite in her mouth.

Satisfied, Charles went back to his meal. They spent the remainder of the meal engaged in light chatter. "Hey, what was it you wanted to talk to me about?" Charles asked, catching Lina off guard.

"I'll tell you later. It's not something I want to share in a crowded restaurant." Lina looked around the room, calling Charles' attention to the other diners seated around them.

"Oh, okay," Charles replied, suddenly noticing the increase in patrons.

Kristen made her way over to their table to check on them. She looked down at their empty plates and asked if they were interested in ordering dessert.

Charles looked over at Lina. She shook her head and raised her palms. "No, I believe we're good. Can you please bring the check?"

Pulling a small black folder from her apron, Kristen placed the check on the side of the table. "Thank you both so much. You can take care of it when you're ready. "

"One second. I'm ready now." Charles reached into his back pocket and pulled out his wallet. He placed several bills in the folder and handed it to the server. "Keep the change."

"Thank you. Enjoy the rest of your day."

Charles stood from the table and helped Lina up. With a wink he smiled and said, "Let's get you home."

Chapter Fourteen

Lina remained oddly silent on the ride home. Charles didn't want to press her. He figured her stomach was bothering her again. He turned on the radio and the car instantly filled with jazzy tunes.

Resting her head on the back of the seat, Lina closed her eyes and prayed silently. Her heart was beating so loud she was sure Charles could hear it. She watched as he drummed his fingers on the steering wheel and bobbed his head as he drove. When Charles made a left turn onto her street she felt her mouth go dry. The moment of truth was approaching fast.

Pulling the car up to the curb, Charles parked in front of Lina's apartment. He stepped around to the passenger side but found Lina had already opened the door. "I would have gotten that for you, sweetheart."

"Oh, I'm sorry. I have a lot on my mind. I didn't even think about it."

"Does this have anything to do with what you need to talk to me about?"

"Yeah, it does," Lina answered honestly. She retrieved her keys from her purse and ascended the stairs to her front door. Unlocking the door, they stepped inside. "Please have a seat. I'll be right back. I need to let Sweetie out of her kennel."

Charles sat with his feet flat on the floor, and his hands resting on his thighs. He looked up with he heard the soft bark of the puppy. Lina held the pooch in her right arm with a leash in her left hand.

"I know I asked you to wait before, but I need to let her out. It will only take a minute. Would you mind waiting a bit longer?"

Charles stood and removed the leash from Lina's hand. "I'll tell you what, let me take her out. That way you can have a few minutes alone to collect your thoughts." Before Lina could debate, Charles took Sweetie from her arms and attached the leash to the small, black harness Sweetie was wearing.

Once Charles and Sweetie were gone, Lina dropped to her knees, clasped her hands, and prayed. *Lord, this is so hard. I never imagined I would be in this place again. I'm afraid of what will happen after I reveal my condition to Charles. Lord, I ask that you give me the strength to talk to him. Give me the words to say. I really like him, but God if he's not the one for me, please show me clearly. This I pray in Jesus name, Amen.*

Rising, Lina wiped the tears that trailed down her face. She hurried to the bathroom to freshen up. The last thing she needed was for Charles to see she had been crying. There was no need to alarm him any more than she already had.

The chime of the doorbell alerted Lina to Charles and Sweetie's return. With a final glance in the mirror, she darted out the bathroom to the front door. "Coming," she called out on her trek. Lina opened the door and Charles pushed Sweetie into her arms.

"I don't know what you've done to this dog, but she is a

little canine diva. I have never had such a hard time taking a dog out. She had the nerve to be picky about where she would go. I've never seen anything like it. When I told her to just pick a place and go, she looked up at me and had the nerve to bark." Charles shook his head and stepped past Lina. "And you say, I'm a mess. Lord, help us all."

"You better leave my baby alone. She knew where she was going." Lina laughed as she closed and locked the front door. She removed the leash and harness from Sweetie and placed her on the floor. Turning to Charles she asked, "Can I get you something to drink?"

"Sure, I'll take some water if you don't mind."

"No problem."

"While you're getting the water, will you point me in the direction of your restroom?"

Lina froze as panic snaked up her spine. Her mind immediately went back to Maxwell finding her medication on the sink. *Ugh, chill out. You're being ridiculous, Lina.* After the incident with Maxwell she never left her meds in the bathroom again. "Uh, sure. It's right this way," she answered, escorting Charles to the hall where the bathroom was located.

Returning to the kitchen, Lina washed her hands and grabbed two bottles of water from the fridge. She walked back to the living room and took a seat on the couch. Her heart pounded when she heard Charles open the bathroom door. "Lord, give me strength," she whispered as his footsteps grew closer.

Charles casually strolled to the couch and took a seat next to Lina. He patted her on the thigh before reaching for the bottle of water on the glass table in front of them. "So, what's going on? What is it you want to talk to me about?"

Lina took Charles' hand and offered him a tight-lipped smile.

"Okay, now you're making me nervous." Pulling his hand from hers, Charles shifted his body so he could look directly into Lina's eyes. "What is it you need to say?" Pausing, he raised his right hand. "Better yet, let me say something first. I really like you, Lina. I've been attracted to you for a long time and I want this," using his index finger he pointed back and forth between him and Lina. "Us, I want us to work out. You're an amazing woman and I believe we can build a good life together."

"Ugh, you are making this so hard. I believe what you're saying is true. I just hope you'll still feel that way after you hear what I have to say." Lina jumped up from the couch and stood on the other side of the table. "First, let me say, I adore you, Charles, and I want nothing more than for us to be together. I've had a crush on you from the moment I met you. No one knew but God and my best friend, Cheri. Never in my wildest imagination did I think we would be here."

"Then what's the problem? We seem to share the same feelings for each other."

Lina plopped down in a chair to the right of the couch. "Charles, I've only been in one serious relationship in my life. A few years ago, I got involved with a guy, but it didn't work out. As for the relationship I was in, it was with a guy I met in college. He was my first love. Anyway, I made the decision to be intimate with him. It was my first, and to be honest only time I've slept with a man."

"So, what are you saying, you're celibate? I'm cool with that."

"Please, let me finish. As I was saying, he's the only one

I've been with. I trusted him, but he betrayed me in the worst way. Kaine took advantage of my love for him and convinced me to have unprotected sex. As a result, I am now HIV positive."

Blood drained from Charles' face. He dropped his head and clasped his hands together.

"I'm telling you this because I like you. If I didn't have this affliction I would be jumping in a relationship with you without question. I dated one other man since Kaine. When he found out about my illness it didn't go well. He later apologized and asked me back, but after the way he treated me, I couldn't be with him. I didn't want to go through that again, nor did I want to put you through it. This way, we're not in too deep. If you want to walk out the door and never look back, I'll understand. The only thing I ask is for you to keep this between us. I don't want people being weird around me."

Charles removed the top from his bottle of water and took a sip. Rising from the couch, he walked over to Lina and pulled her up from the chair into an embrace. "Thank you for telling me." He wanted to say more, but the words wouldn't come.

Chapter Fifteen

"HIV! She has HIV!" Charles banged his hand on the steering wheel. He started the car and pulled away from the curb. When Lina said she needed to tell him something a million thoughts raced through his mind. Never in his wildest imagination did he think she would tell him she had HIV. When she started talking about having unprotected sex and only being with one guy his mind went from thinking she'd had an abortion, to a secret child somewhere. He even entertained the thought that maybe she was into women, a thought which he quickly dismissed. Anything but this.

Charles drove in the direction of his home but reconsidered. He needed to talk to someone and there was only one person he could go to. Making a right turn, he drove down Garfield Boulevard to South Wells Street. With another right turn he merged onto the Dan Ryan expressway heading to the suburb of Calumet City.

"Nephew, what are you doing here?" India stepped aside and allowed Charles to enter her duplex apartment.

"You kill me calling me Nephew. We're only two years apart, India." Moving past his aunt, Charles headed straight for the kitchen as if he hadn't recently eaten. "What do you have to eat in here?"

"Get your greedy self out of my kitchen. I know you didn't drive all the way out here just to see what I have to eat. You're usually at home chillin' or out with somebody at this time." India scanned Charles' wardrobe. She noticed the cuffed white dress shirt, charcoal gray vest, and black slacks. Frowning, she continued in an elevated tone. "Plus, you still have your church clothes on. What's going on?"

Charles pulled a plate out of the cabinet and retrieved a fork from the dish rack. "Man, it's bad. I got some devastating news from somebody I care about today and I don't know how to handle it." Removing the lid from a large pot on the stove, Charles scooped out spaghetti and added it to his plate. He peeled back aluminum foil from a glass rectangular baking dish and placed two small fried catfish filets on his plate. Pulling down a loaf of bread from the top of the refrigerator he opened the package and removed a slice. He opened the fridge and grabbed a bottle of Coke.

Moving from the kitchen, he walked to the dining room and sat his plate on the table. "Where's the hot sauce?" Charles asked India as he pulled a chair from the table and took a seat.

"Ain't no maids around here. The hot sauce is in the cabinet. You got everything else, you can get that too."

"Come on, India, stop trippin'. Hand me the hot sauce. Who'd you cook all this food for anyway. You're the only one here."

India slammed the bottle of hot sauce down on the table. "I cooked it for me and my man, if you must know. He'll be here soon." She pulled out a chair and sat across from Charles. "Stop stalling and tell me what's up with you."

Charles opened the hot sauce and sprinkled it over his food. He felt bad for betraying Lina's trust but he couldn't deal with it alone. Using the side of his fork, he cut into the fish and placed the bite in his mouth. Charles chewed quickly when he saw India's look of frustration. "There's this woman I've been interested in for quite some time. I couldn't date her because she worked for me, but she no longer does. Anyway, I've been seeing her for a couple of weeks. This is the type of woman I want to spend the rest of my life with."

"Then what's the problem?" India asked, failing to see the issue.

"Today she told me she's sick." Charles dropped his fork on the plate, making a loud clanking sound.

"What do you mean sick? You need to give me a little more information. Saying she's sick is a pretty broad statement.

Charles looked deep into his aunt's eyes. "She has HIV, India."

"Oh," India replied, lowering her eyes. "How did she contract the virus?"

"She told me she was a virgin, and her first boyfriend convinced her to have unprotected sex, the first and according to her only time they slept together."

"You talk like you don't believe her."

"I'm not saying I don't believe her, it's just a lot to digest."

"Where is the guy now? Is he still around?"

"He's dead." Picking his fork up, Charles filled it with spaghetti and shoved it in his mouth.

"What! Did she kill him?"

"Nah, she said this dude went around infecting a bunch

of women. Apparently one of the other women he infected killed him."

"I can see how it could happen. God knows I wanted to kill the guy that infected me."

"You and me both. He'd better be glad we couldn't find him because our whole family was on the hunt for him.

India pushed her chair back and stood. "What is it you want me to say, Charles? I mean, I may be bias seeing as though I've been living with HIV since I was sixteen. This disease isn't new to you. You've watched me deal with it. Shoot, you stood by my side more than anybody." India walked over to Charles and placed her hand on his shoulder. "You were the one who convinced me my life wasn't over. I'll never forget when you said this disease didn't define me."

"That was different, India."

"Different how? Are you saying my life is more important than the woman you said you could see yourself with for the rest of your life?"

"India, I want to have children one day. Look, I'm a man. I'm gon' keep it real with you. I can't imagine having to wrap it up for the rest of my life, especially if I'm married."

Stepping away from Charles, India asked, "What if it were you? Would you want her to stand by you? Nobody infected with HIV asked for this disease. However, there are people living full, productive lives despite having it. Several of my friends from the support group are involved in relationships where their significant others are HIV negative. Some of them have had children too and their children are negative. When the infected person is faithful to taking antiretroviral medications the risk of transmitting the disease is much lower."

Charles stood and cleared his dishes from the table. "What are you saying? I should be with her?"

"I wouldn't dare make a decision like that for you. Only you can decide how to move forward now that you know. All I'm saying is it's not the end of the world. You're into church. Pray about it."

Chapter Sixteen

Lina scrolled through her recent contacts and selected Cheri's phone number. She pressed the button to place the call. Her heart was aching. She needed her best friend like never before. Tears stained her face. Dark circles from her ruined mascara gave her a raccoon like appearance. Sweetie nuzzled up against her foot as she sat on the edge of her bed. Cheri answered Lina's call on the second ring.

"Hey, Lina. How're you doing, girl?"

Skipping all formalities, Lina cried into the phone. "I told him."

"Hold on a second." The sound became muffled as Cheri covered the phone with her hand. *Babe, give me a minute I need to take this call.* Cheri went into her bedroom and closed the door. She returned to the phone after a brief pause. "Okay, I'm alone now. What happened? What did he say?"

"Oh, Cheri. I don't know. He was calm while I was telling him. Almost too calm, which seemed weird at first, but then again, he's always calm. He was the same way at work. I told him everything from me being a virgin and only sleeping with Kaine once to my cousin telling me Kaine had been killed. I put it all out there. I even told him about what happened with Maxwell and how he acted a fool with me and then came back wanting to be with me. He listened to everything I had to say then he gave me a hug and left. He said he'll call me, but to be honest I don't expect to hear from him again. I hope he doesn't tell anyone what I told him."

"You know what? You don't need to be alone right now. I'm coming over. Give me about fifteen minutes."

"Okay," Lina uttered between sobs. She was happy her best friend lived close by, especially in times such as this one. Being in a city with no family and only one close friend, she was grateful for the support Cheri gave.

Lina went to the bathroom and washed her face. In the time since Charles left she had been a blubbering mess. Once she was satisfied with her appearance she went into the kitchen to make a fresh pitcher of iced tea. She needed something to occupy her mind and rein in her thoughts. Pausing, Lina placed both of her palms on the counter, closed her eyes, and took a deep breath.

The doorbell rang, pulling her from her moment of serenity. Sweetie barked in response to the familiar ding and rushed to the door. Leaping on her hind legs, she stuck out her tongue and panted as Lina opened the door. Seeing her best friend standing at the door induced a fresh round of tears for Lina.

"Aw, honey. Come here," Cheri said, pulling Lina into her arms. She used her foot to close the door. The friends stood without saying a word as Lina leaned on Cheri's shoulder. Cheri patted her on the back while Sweetie nuzzled against her leg.

"I don't know what to do," Lina uttered between sobs as she lifted her head.

Reaching back, Cheri locked the front door before walking over with Lina to the couch. "Tell me what happened. Start from the beginning."

"You want something to eat or drink?" Lina asked, rising from the couch.

"I'm fine. Tell me what happened." Cheri pulled on Lina's arm, urging her to sit back down.

"Like I was telling you on the phone, he and I went to church together earlier. I knew after spending time with him yesterday it was time to tell him my status. Being with him today further confirmed it. We went to church and had a great time. Before the service was over, I knew my feelings for him were growing stronger."

Cheri furrowed her eyebrows in confusion. "Did he tell you he doesn't want to see you anymore? I mean, how do you know things are not going to work out?"

"He didn't tell me anything. He hugged me and thanked me for telling him. Then he asked about Kaine. After I told him Kaine was killed by one of the women he infected with the virus, he made an excuse to leave. He said something about needing to go home and get ready for a business trip. He never mentioned a business trip before and we've talked practically every day for the past few weeks."

"Don't go jumping to conclusions. Maybe he does have a business trip planned. Let's give him the benefit of the doubt."

"Whose side are you on, Cheri?"

"It's not about taking sides. I just don't want you to be too hard on the man. You have to know what you told him was a lot to take in. Give him a little time to process it. If he's for you, he'll come around. If he's not, at least you wouldn't have invested as much time as you did with Maxwell."

Lina considered her friend's words. She didn't want

to be selfish, but she also didn't want to be hurt. Cheri was right. Before becoming involved, she and Charles had maintained a good working relationship. He already had treated her better than Maxwell did when he found out her status.

"Tell you what," Cheri cut into Lina's thoughts. "Let's go to the movies. You need to get out of this apartment and focus on something other than the conversation you had with Charles. You've been saying you want to see the new comedy everyone is talking about. I think this is the best time to go. Get your purse. I'll drive."

Lina and Cheri exited the theater still laughing at the film they had watched. "Girl, that man is a straight up fool. I'm so glad we decided to do this. I needed the getaway," Lina said, remaining in step with Cheri. "It's still early. We might as well walk the mall while we're here."

Cheri and Lina were looking at each other talking as they made their way to the theater's exit. Cheri bumped into a man, practically knocking a bucket of popcorn out of his hands. "Excuse me, I'm so sorry," Cheri pleaded, looking up at the man for the first time. "Minister Lee. Hey, how are you?"

"I'm good. How are you, Sister Cheri?"

"I'm doing real good, Minister Lee," Cheri replied with a slight smirk.

"Actually, it's *Pastor* Lee, now," Maxwell replied, focusing his attention on Lina.

"Oh, my bad. I did hear you were the pastor now. I meant no disrespect." Cheri was very much aware of Maxwell's position as pastor. She called him Minister Lee to test him.

She wanted to know if he was still as cocky as he was when she was a member of Christ the True Vine church.

"Not a problem." Maxwell spoke to Cheri but continued to focus on Lina. "How are you, Lina?"

"I'm well, thank you."

"Hello, ladies, how are you?" Amirah asked, walking up and interrupting the reunion. Her lips held a smile her eyes didn't reflect. "Ms. Fairweather, how nice to see you, *again*."

"You too, Amirah."

"Thank you again for the photos. I was very pleased with how well they turned out. You are truly a skilled photographer."

"You're welcome. I'm glad you liked them."

Amirah shifted her stance and turned her focus to Cheri. "I'm sorry. I don't believe we've met. I'm Amirah, Pastor Lee's wife." Placing her hand on Maxwell's chest, she affirmed her position.

Maxwell spoke up. "Uh, baby, this is Sister Cheri. She used to be a member of the church as well."

Patting Maxwell on the chest, Amirah held her tight smile. "We seem to be meeting a lot of *ex* members lately." Amirah stressed the word ex.

Cheri looked at Lina, then back at the couple. Matching Amirah's smile, she said, "Well, if you all will excuse us, we were heading out."

"Oh, you're leaving," Amirah said as more of a statement than a question.

Cheri spoke up, unfazed by Amirah. "Yes, we're leaving. Enjoy your movie." In an act of defiance, Cheri reached into Maxwell's bucket and grabbed a few kernels of popcorn. Leaving both Maxwell and Amirah stunned.

Chapter Seventeen

"This is ridiculous. What in the world is going on, Maxwell?" Amirah yelled to the top of her lungs as Maxwell steered the car down the street.

"Amirah, you need to calm down. Like I told you at the theater, there is nothing going on."

"That's a load of crap and you know it. I saw the way you were looking at Lina. If you're not involved with her now, you have been in the past."

"What are you talking about? I didn't look at her in any particular way. I was standing there talking to the both of them, the same as I do with any of my members, both past and present." Maxwell purposely avoided confirming his past relationship with Lina.

Amirah folded her arms and crossed her legs in the spacious passenger seat. "You must think I'm stupid. I saw you long before you realized I was there. You were talking to Cheri, but you didn't take your eyes off Lina. When I stepped up, you practically started stuttering. I almost had to ask for an introduction."

"That's nonsense. I've told you there is nothing going on between me and Lina or any other woman for that matter. You are the only woman I want. Don't start being insecure. You have nothing to worry about. Let's enjoy the rest of our evening, please." Maxwell turned on the radio and tuned in to the gospel station, signaling to Amirah he was finished with their conversation.

Amirah fumed but didn't press. She didn't care what Maxwell said, she was no idiot. The words of her grandmother rang in her ears as clearly as the day she'd spoken them. *A woman knows when there's something going on between her man and another woman, be it past, present, or future. Don't you let that little church title of yours cause you to forget who you are. Just because you become a first lady it doesn't make you a dummy.*

Although the words were spoken to Amirah's mother when Amirah was a child, she'd held on to them and pondered them in her heart. Amirah watched the heartache, despair, and embarrassment her mother endured throughout the many years her father served as pastor of Holy Zion Baptist Church. They always seemed to take a back seat to whatever the church had going on.

The last position Amirah ever wanted to hold was first lady. She could do without the spotlight and the expectation to share her husband. She met Maxwell while working at Mercy Hospital as a registered nurse. His mother had been admitted to the hospital for pneumonia. Amirah was in charge of her care. Working twelve to sixteen hour shifts, there was plenty of time for Maxwell to see Amirah. By the time his mother was released, Amirah and Maxwell had spent hours together talking and getting to know one another.

Six months into their relationship, Maxwell asked her to marry him. Amirah knew he was a minister, but she figured his focus was on his clothing store and not on being a pastor. She learned of his plans to take over as pastor of Christ the True Vine during one of their premarital counseling sessions. By then she'd allowed her heart to overrule any reservations she had. She loved Maxwell and wanted nothing more than to be his wife. She also thought the role of Pastor and First Lady was in their distant future. Her work schedule prevented her from attending the Sunday services which further hindered her knowledge of just how quickly her life would change.

Before the ink was dry on their marriage license, Maxwell was installed as Pastor of Christ the True Vine Church. He convinced her their life wouldn't change. He promised he would always put her first and never neglect her needs as his wife. Initially, Maxwell kept his promises. He was an attentive husband. He'd also made a point to carve out time from his schedule to spend with her.

Now, only a few months later, things were changing so fast she could hardly keep up. The first blow came when Maxwell convinced her to quit her nursing job. He told her it would give them freedom as a couple, allowing them to travel without restriction. The part he didn't tell her was the travel would predominantly be church related.

The next thing he hit her with was his desire for her to work in the church, taking over various administrative tasks and leading a women's Bible study group. Now, the so-called former church members were springing up like oil in Texas. Regardless of what he said, she was convinced Maxwell had some kind of involvement with Lina Fairweather. His mouth spoke one thing, but his eyes revealed the lies his lips told. Her life had taken a rapid turn from marital bliss to *First Lady Blues*.

Maxwell and Amirah continued the remainder of the drive home without speaking. As hard as she fought, she was unable to stop the tears from falling. She shifted her body to the right until she was facing the window.

Pulling into the garage, Maxwell turned to her. "Amirah, what's wrong? Why are you crying?" He reached for her, but she pulled away.

"Why won't you tell me the truth? I know there's something more between you and Ms. Fairweather than what you're telling."

"Baby, you don't have anything to worry about. I told you, I don't want anybody but you. Hear me when I tell you, I'm not trying to go there. That woman has AIDS."

"What!" Cheri snapped her head around so fast her neck made a popping sound.

"You heard me. She's HIV positive. Why would I risk losing my beautiful, healthy wife whom I love with all that's in me for her? I would never do that to you, myself, or my ministry. It's not worth it."

Amirah sat stunned. Surely, Maxwell wouldn't go to the extreme of saying Lina was HIV positive to cover up an affair. It was time for her to do a little investigating. If what he said was true, she would leave it alone. If it turned out he was lying, he would regret it.

Chapter Eighteen

The buzz of the cell phone jarred Lina from her sleep. She glanced at the clock on the night table before slapping the phone and knocking it to the floor. Her frustration mounted as the phone continued to buzz. Whoever was on the other end was going to get a piece of her mind. Everyone knew she treasured her sleep and didn't like to be awakened unless it was a dire emergency.

"What?" she answered in a groggy tone without focusing on the name of the caller. She squinted, hoping the brightness of the phone wouldn't rouse her too much.

"Lina? I'm sorry. Did I wake you?"

"Yes, you woke me. It's a quarter past midnight. Who is this?" she moaned.

"It's Charles. I didn't mean to wake you. I keep forgetting about the time difference."

Lina sat up in the bed, pulling her knees close to her chest. "Time difference, where are you?"

"I'm in Los Angeles. I thought I told you Sunday I had to go out of town on business. I would have called you sooner, but the company has kept me quite busy since I arrived on the west coast."

"You really did have a business meeting?"

"Of course, I did. What, did you think I was lying? I would never lie to you."

"I just thought, since I...after I, I thought, maybe. You never mentioned going out of town on business before Sunday afternoon. I thought you were using it as your exit strategy," Lina stammered. She didn't want to mention their previous conversation, but she knew he was aware of why she thought he'd lied.

Charles continued the conversation as if the moment they shared wasn't awkward. "Listen, I know it's late and I clearly interrupted your sleep. I'll be back in town tomorrow. I was hoping we could get together for dinner or something. Say around six."

"Oh, okay. Dinner will be fine."

"Cool. I'll call you tomorrow. Goodnight, Lina."

"Goodnight, Charles." Lina stared at the phone long after Charles ended the call. Her mind was going in so many directions. She pinched her arm then squealed from the pain. She had to make sure she wasn't dreaming. As much as she wanted to, she couldn't figure Charles out.

Lina hadn't communicated with Charles in three days. Initially, the lack of communication bothered her. After the first full day of not hearing from him she comforted herself by saying perhaps he needed some time to think. When he hadn't called or texted on the second day her confidence started to waver. By the third day of not hearing anything from Charles, Lina decided it was time to move on and focus her attention elsewhere. She surmised she was comfortable with her life as it was and would be content with enjoying her life as a single woman.

Sitting up in the middle of the bed, Lina wished for sleep but knew it wouldn't return. She had allowed herself to come to grips with not being with Charles and now here she was faced with all of the emotions once again. She pushed the covers back and stood. Taking familiar steps, she went into the dark kitchen and retrieved a bottle of water from the fridge. Lastly , she made her way to the couch, grabbed the TV remote, and clicked the power button.

Lina scanned the channels until she found a movie that caught her attention. She pulled her legs up on the couch and wrapped up in the warmth of the chenille throw she kept on the back of the couch. Her mind drifted easily to Charles but she forced the thoughts to the back of her mind. She was determined whatever was meant to happen would happen. Focusing her attention on the movie, Lina watched until Charles was no longer consuming her thoughts.

Rays of light emerged through the living room windows ushering in the new day. Lina stretched her body and massaged the ache in her neck. She hadn't intended to fall asleep on the couch. When she felt her body drifting into the welcomed slumber she surrendered. The dawning of the day brought along with it the anxiety of her pending dinner date with Charles.

Dropping to her knees, Lina spoke a prayer of thanks for a new day. She asked the Lord for guidance and protection. Lina had barely uttered Amen before Sweetie made her way to Lina's side. She greeted the pooch and moved on to her private bathroom. She hoped the massaging shower head and hot water would ease the muscle aches she gained after sleeping on the couch.

Thoughts of Charles once again consumed her. Rather than think about him in a negative way, Lina chose to focus on what could be. She allowed her mind to drift to the scent of his cologne, and the hardness of his muscular body. She recalled the warmth of his touch when he held her hand, and the tenderness of his kiss against her cheek.

Lina longed to be normal. Resisting the urge to become angry she chose to imagine a different reality. She wondered what life would have been like for her and Charles if she wasn't faced with the affliction in her body. Thoughts of his lips hungrily covering hers caused goosebumps to appear on her skin. Butterflies danced in her belly as she pictured him holding her close, heart to heart and skin to skin. She placed her hand on her toned abdomen and imagined it stretching to accommodate a life growing inside. The length of her shower caused the water to run cold snapping her back to the present.

Grabbing a towel from the rack, Lina dried off and made her way to her bedroom. She dressed in athletic gear and sent a text message to Cheri. They agreed to meet at the gym. Lina couldn't wait to tell Cheri about her pending date with Charles. She was sure her friend would have a strong opinion.

Chapter Nineteen

Charles arrived at Lina's apartment at six o'clock on the dot. He rang the bell and patiently waited for her to answer. He didn't know how receptive she would be considering he'd left her hanging for several days. It didn't take a genius to know the way he handled things left much to be desired. Given the facts, he was surprised Lina had agreed to meet him for dinner. Nonetheless, he was grateful she had.

The door opened and Lina stood before him more beautiful than he remembered. The silky iridescent dress she wore shimmered in the blowing wind. Her hair was pinned to one side, revealing an elegant neckline he wanted to plant kisses on. Lina's toned arms rivaled those of Michele Obama's. Natural makeup tones further enhanced her beauty with glossy peach lips topping off the look.

"You look amazing," Charles complimented. Spotting the small teal handbag that matched her stilettos hanging from her right shoulder, he knew she would not be inviting him in. He asked the question for which he already knew the answer. "Are you ready to go?"

"I sure am," Lina said as she stepped outside, closed, and locked her door.

Notable surprise registered on Charles' face when Lina declined to take his extended arm. She patted him on the arm and clutched her purse with both hands. When they arrived at his car she stepped aside and allowed him to open her door. She slid into the seat. Charles closed the door and stepped around the car. He looked up at the sky with a nonverbal plea for help. Charles knew he'd hurt Lina, still he hoped for her understanding.

"I made reservations at Morton's downtown. Have you ever eaten there?"

"No, but I've heard of it. I'm looking forward to trying it," she answered.

Wanting to make the evening as less awkward as possible, Charles talked about his trip to Los Angeles. He was relieved when Lina opened up and joined in the conversation. He couldn't stand the obvious tension that had settled between them. Talk of work filled the space between them until they arrived at the restaurant.

Lina appeared more relaxed as she accepted the arm she had previously declined. Relief swept over Charles' features. He escorted her into the restaurant in hopes of a quiet, uneventful meal. The crowd was relatively light, allowing them to be seated right away. Charles pulled out the padded leather chair for Lina before taking his seat.

He ordered two glasses of Butter Block, Chardonnay and asked the server to give them time to look over the menus.

"This place is elegant," Lina said, speaking of the opulent décor that filled the dining room. The soft lighting gave the restaurant a romantic feel. Photos of celebrity diners were displayed neatly on the walls, drawing Lina's attention. She picked up a large cloth napkin and placed it across her lap.

"I agree, it is nice. I just hope the food lives up to the hype. All this elegance won't mean a thing if the food isn't good. This restaurant claims to have the best steaks in Chicago. We shall see." Charles opened the menu and scanned its contents. "I'm going to try the center-cut prime ribeye with the grilled jumbo asparagus. What about you?"

"I think I'll go with the honey balsamic glazed salmon fillet and the creamed spinach."

The server returned with the glasses of wine and took their dinner orders. Charles swirled the wine around in his glass before taking a sip. A weight hung over him, reminding him he could no longer avoid the necessary conversation between him and Lina.

"I really appreciate you agreeing to have dinner with me. I realize you could have easily said no."

"Why would I say no to dinner? We're friends, right?" Lina's tone was laced with sarcasm.

"Of course, we are. Nothing and no one will ever come between our friendship. It's just that the last conversation we had was deep. You gave me a lot to think about. It's not every day someone shares with me the news you shared." Charles paused, examining Lina's features. Her blank expression urged him to continue. "To be honest, I needed a moment to process everything. I won't lie, I know I was wrong for not contacting you for a few days. Even though I was busy with work I could've reached out."

"I know this is difficult for you, Charles. You were well within your rights to distance yourself. I was actually surprised when you called. After the first couple of days of not hearing from you I thought that pretty much sealed it. By the third day I thought I'd never hear from you again. When I received the phone call at midnight I never expected it to be your voice on the other end. Now, I don't forgive you for breaking my sleep, and I will caution you to never do that again unless of course you're half dead.

Other than that, there's no reason for forgiveness."

The server returned with their meals and stepped away from the table. Charles stretched his hand across the table with his palm up, beckoning Lina to place her hand in his. She complied and they bowed their heads while Charles prayed a blessing over the food.

"Let me see if this steak is all they say it is." Charles peeled a portion of his steak off using his fork. "Ooh wee, baby. That's one tender steak." He cut off a second piece and reached over to Lina, urging her to take a bite.

Lina looked at the fork like there was a live snake on the end of it. "What are you doing?" she whispered.

"I want you to taste my steak. Open your mouth." He whirled the fork around like a parent trying to feed a child.

Tapping her own plate with her fork Lina said, "Put it here, and I'll taste it."

"Sweetheart, open up. The steak is getting cold," he pressed.

"You want me to eat off your fork?"

"Yes, I wouldn't be sitting here catching a cramp in my arm holding the fork up if I didn't. Now will you please take the bite."

Lina leaned forward and bit into the meat, pulling it off the fork. She was careful not to touch his fork with her mouth. She nodded as she chewed. "Um, that is good."

"Let me try your salmon," Charles said, and pointed at the fish with his fork.

"No," Lina said with finality. "Now will you please finish your meal without drawing any more attention to us?"

"Humph," Charles pouted, causing Lina to giggle. "There's the smile I've been missing all night. Did you know when you smile your nostrils flare a little?"

"They do not," she insisted, covering her nose with her napkin.

"Yeah, they do. It's very subtle, but it's cute. I like it."

The more they talked, the more relaxed Lina became. Soon she was chattering as if there was never any tension between them. Charles could tell Lina was enjoying his company. He had to admit in the three days he didn't communicate with her, he missed her. Lina brought things out in him no other woman had. When they were together there was a feeling of security. He didn't have to wonder if she had ulterior motives. It was as if his company was enough for her. Despite her status, he knew he didn't want to be without Lina.

Charles patted his swollen belly. "That was a good meal. I'm glad we came here." Lina nodded in agreement. The server brought their check and attempted to lay it on the table. "Don't go anywhere please. We're ready to leave." He handed the server his credit card and watched as the man scurried away.

"Thank you for dinner," Lina said, taking a final sip of her wine.

"My pleasure," Charles replied in a deeper than normal tone.

The waiter returned with a pen and the folder containing two receipts. Charles scribbled the tip amount on the receipt, signed it, and handed the pen and folder back to the server. "Thank you so much for dining with us this evening. We look forward to seeing you again."

"Are you ready to go, sweetheart?" Charles asked Lina before standing.

"Um hmm," she replied in a hum. Lina placed her hand in Charles' hand as he lifted her from her seat.

He put his hand on the small of her back, ushering her to the door. "Would you mind if we parked at the lake for a little while? I have something I need to say to you and I'd rather it be in private."

"Sure, that'll be fine."

Lina's breathing increased, displaying obvious tension. Charles knew he could no longer prolong things. It was time to get everything out in the open so they could move forward with their lives. It was time for him to tell Lina how he felt.

Chapter Twenty

Lina's heart pounded against her chest. The entire night had led up to this moment. She hadn't missed the terms of endearment Charles was using on her, calling her baby and sweetheart. Those names wouldn't mean a thing if he was about to tell her he didn't want to see her anymore. One thing was for sure, it would be horrible of him to show her such a beautiful evening before giving her the boot.

Smoothing imaginary wrinkles out of her dress, Lina thought about the advice Cheri had given her at the gym. *Girl, you better make sure when that man sees you tonight his eyes pop out of his head. Put on your sexiest dress, pull your hair up, and put on some makeup. Don't make it slutty, make it classy. One thing is for sure, if he is breaking things off you'll give him something to remember. Trust me, his decision won't be an easy one. Let him know what he'll be missing out on.*

She'd followed her friend's advice to the letter. It was obvious when she opened the door for him, Charles wasn't expecting her to look the way she did. Lina had been tense for several days. First there was tension from him not knowing her status, followed by tension when she shared her status with him and now more tension waiting on his decision. If Charles stalled any longer Lina didn't know what she would do.

Charles pulled the car up to a parking area near the lakefront and turned off the engine. He lowered the windows, allowing the calming sounds of the water and the wind to flow through the vehicle.

Lina folded her hands in her lap and took a deep breath. All of the stalling was weighing heavily on her. "Charles."

He held his hand up, silencing her. "If you don't mind, I would like to go first. We've had a wonderful evening so far, but we both know there is a pressing matter between us that has to be dealt with." Charles blew out a breath. "When you told me to remind you to tell me something, I never expected it to be your HIV status. Especially a positive status. I was focusing on how we could move our relationship further along, but you dropped a bomb."

"I had to tell you, Charles. I couldn't live with secrets between us."

"I appreciated your honesty but I needed time to deal with it all. There was a lot left unsaid when I left your apartment Sunday. I don't want you to think your status has changed my opinion of you as a woman in any way because it hasn't. Someone close to me is also living with the disease so I'm more familiar with it than you would think. The difference is the person is a relative and not someone I want to have an intimate relationship with."

Lina opened her mouth to speak, but she didn't know what to say.

"During our time apart, I did a lot of praying and a lot of research. I learned a lot. Things I never realized about HIV and people living with it." Charles shifted in his seat, turning to face Lina. "Here's the thing. I had to decide if HIV was a good enough reason to not be with the woman I've already imagined a future with. The answer was no. It's not. At this point, I can't think of anything worth me *not* being with you. You're the woman I desire, and with the Lord's help, I believe we can get through this."

"Charles, do you really feel this way? Are you serious?" Lina couldn't believe the words he was speaking. Could he really be saying he still wanted to be with her even though she was HIV positive? This had to be a dream. There was no way it could be real.

"Yes, Lina, I mean every word. I'm in love with you." Charles placed his hand on the back of Lina's neck and pulled her closer to him. For the first time, he covered her mouth with his and kissed her passionately.

Lina had barely crossed the threshold of her apartment before she was on the phone calling Cheri. She was still reeling from her interaction with Charles. Their first kiss sent an electric charge through her that could only be compared to hospital paddles used to jump start the heart of a patient.

Cheri answered on the third ring, sounding a bit preoccupied. "Hey girl, what's up?" she asked in a hushed tone.

"Did I catch you at a bad time?"

"Yes, you did." Lina heard David call out in the background.

"Shhh, stop playing," Cheri said to David. She turned her attention back to Lina. "Go ahead, Lina. What's going on?"

"I was calling to tell you about my date with Charles, but I can tell you later. I know David gets tired of me pulling you away from him with my drama. Go back to your man, we can talk later."

"Girl, please. He ain't going nowhere. Tell me about your date."

"Okay, but I'll make it as quick as possible." Lina didn't want to cause a rift in Cheri's relationship, but she was desperate to share her news with someone. "When he first picked me up I had a major attitude and I didn't try to hide it. I felt justified because he did leave me hanging for several days after all."

"I agree. Any woman or man for that matter would have been upset, given the circumstances. You can't disappear off the face of the earth without a trace and then pop back up like nothing happened."

"My thoughts exactly. Anyway, when he saw how good I was looking he was stunned into silence." Lina described her outfit to Cheri in full detail.

"See, that's what I'm talking about. Let him know what he's dealing with."

"Umm hmmm," Lina purred her agreement. "We went to dinner, which was delicious. I'll have to tell you about the restaurant another time."

"Did y'all talk at all?" Cheri asked, growing impatient.

"I'm getting to that part."

"Can you get there a little quicker. You're holding up progress on this end," David interjected once again.

"David, stop," Cheri chastised. "Go on, Lina. I'm listening."

"Okay, let me hurry up before your man stops letting you talk to me," she teased. "I'll skip to the good part. Girl, Charles took me to the lake and we sat in his car and talked. He apologized for not talking to me sooner. He was wrong and he knew it. "He told me he weighed his options and he realized there was nothing worth losing me over.

Despite my situation, he chose me. Cheri, he told me he's in love with me and girl he sealed his declaration with a kiss. I'm not talking about a peck on the cheek. He gave me a real passionate kiss. The kind I haven't experienced since I was with Kaine. Except this was better, way better than I remembered or even imagined."

"Oh, my God, Lina. I'm so happy for you. I told you God would send the right man to you. I knew it. Girl, you got me up here crying." Cheri wiped her cheek where a single tear trailed down her face. "You deserve it, Lina."

"Thank you, bestie. I'm still in a bit of shock but I'm so happy. I believe the worst part is behind us."

"I hope so, but you can never get too comfortable. It's been a long time since you've been in a real relationship, and honey let me tell you they take work. This is only the beginning for you and Charles. Let's see where it leads."

Chapter Twenty-One

Hey, baby, it's Charles. I guess you must be working. Give me a call when you get a free moment. I want to talk to you about something. Take care, sweetheart.

Lina played the voicemail message from Charles a few times before placing her phone back inside her bag. She was in the middle of a major photo shoot with the cast of an urban film being shot in Chicago. The cast was filled with A-list celebrities including Academy Award winning actress Essence Journey. She didn't have time to answer nor return Charles' phone call.

It still amazed Lina at how close she and Charles had become in such a short amount of time. They had only been officially dating for a month but it felt like they had been together for years. Lina wrapped her shoot and dialed Charles at the office.

"Good afternoon, you've reached Mr. Davenport's office. How may I assist you?"

"Hi, Lindsey. Is Charles available?"

"Oh, hi, Ms. Fairweather. I believe he's available. Give me just a moment and I'll check for you." Lindsey, Charles' assistant, placed the call on hold. Classical music played softly on the line while Lina waited. "One moment, Ms. Fairweather. I'll put you through."

The phone rang once before Lina heard Charles on

the other end. "Hey, sweetheart. Thanks for calling me back. How are things going? You had a big shoot today, didn't you?" Charles showed genuine interest in Lina's work, which she loved. He believed she was an excellent photographer, which is why he'd hired her at *About Us* magazine.

"Yeah, I did. We wrapped about fifteen minutes ago. You wanted me to call you. What's up?"

"I was calling to see if you had plans for this evening. I have somewhere very important I would like to take you."

"You know I'm not big on surprises. I'm free, but I want to know where we're going."

"Tell you what, I'll let you know where we're going when I pick you up. Right now, I have to go. I have a meeting starting in a few minutes."

"Charles," Lina moaned to deaf ears. Charles had already disconnected the call. She stared at the phone before tossing it in her bag. Looking at her watch she realized she was running late for her lunch with Cheri.

Lina entered the restaurant and looked around for Cheri. Figuring she hadn't arrived yet, Lina pulled out her phone to give her a call.

"Ms. Fairweather, how are you?"

Turning her attention away from the phone, Lina looked up to find Amirah Lee standing before her. Seeing Maxwell's wife, she was glad her friend hadn't arrived. The last time they had seen each other it didn't go well, especially when Cheri took popcorn from Maxwell's bucket.

"Amirah, what a pleasant surprise. How are you?" Lina tried to sound as lighthearted as possible.

"I'm doing well. In fact, I'm glad I bumped into you. I

think we need to talk."

"Talk? About what?" Lina struggled to keep the irritation from her voice. Based on Amirah's tone and body language, Lina was well aware of what Amirah wanted to talk about, however it was a subject she wasn't the least bit interested in.

"I think you know without me having to say. I want to know the extent of your relationship with my husband. We've already had two random, awkward moments involving you, him, and me. I'm no fool. I've seen the way he looks at you, and it's not the kind of look you give to a regular church member. Is there something going on between you and Maxwell?"

Lina took a step back. The more Amirah spoke, the further into Lina's personal space she broached. "Look, Amirah, there isn't anything going on between me and your husband. I, for one, would never get involved with a married man."

Amirah placed her hand on her hip. "Say I believe you. There's nothing going on between you and Maxwell *now*. I'll buy that. You only answered part of my question. You and Maxwell have some obvious history and it's not as simple as minister and church member. So please don't insult my intelligence."

"Whoa, your hostility is unwarranted. Why are you confronting me with this anyway? Maxwell is your husband. This is a discussion you should be having with him, not me."

"He told me you have AIDS. Is that true?"

"You know what, I don't have the time or the patience to deal with this mess. Whatever issues you and your husband have are not because of me. Now, if you will excuse me."

"Answer the question," Amirah said, blocking Lina.

"Nothing about me is of your concern. Now, I'm not going to tell you again, move and leave me alone." Lina pushed past Amirah, practically knocking her over. She made it to the door, just as Cheri was walking in.

"I'm going to find out the truth. You better stay away from my man," Amirah called out, not caring who may have recognized her.

"Hey, Lina, what's going on?" Cheri asked when she saw the scowl on Lina's face.

"I've suddenly lost my appetite. Let's go," Lina replied, looking over her shoulder and turning her nose up at Amirah.

Cheri looked over and noticed Amirah for the first time since entering the restaurant. She looked back to find her friend but saw she had already left the restaurant. "Lina, wait up," Cheri called out, once she was outside.

Lina quickened her pace, causing Cheri to run to catch up to her. "What in the world has you so upset?" Cheri asked, catching her breath.

"I had to get out of there before I knocked that woman out." Lina spoke so fast her words started to run together. "Calling herself confronting me about Maxwell. That is her man, and therefore her problem. Ugh, why can't I seem to shake that man and all things related to him. I closed that door a long time ago and he and his crazy wife keep opening it." Lina turned to face Cheri with tears in her eyes. "Do you know she had the nerve to tell me that bastard told her I have AIDS. I mean really, how low can he get?"

Cheri put her arms around Lina who wept openly in her arms. "Come on, Lina. Don't let them get to you. It doesn't matter what he says about you to try to cover up his feelings, because you know he still has feelings for you. I could tell when we saw him at the movie theater he's not over you."

"I couldn't care less. Getting out of his car that day he came to my job was the best decision I could have made. He is a no-good, dirty dog who does and says whatever he can to benefit himself. He is so selfish."

"Listen, Lina. Stop this. Maxwell and his wife are irrelevant. Don't give them power over you by letting them get to you like this. You have far too much going for you. You don't have time for this nonsense."

"I know you're right, Cheri. I could've handled her little confrontation, but I wasn't prepared for her asking if I have AIDS. That was an unnecessary blow and you know it."

"Yes, it was but you can't let that moment define you. This is not the first time you've dealt with Maxwell or someone associated with him in this way. Sad to say, it may not be the last time. Only God knows. It's not how they treat you that matters, it's how you respond." Cheri pointed her toward a different restaurant. "I don't know about you but I'm hungry and I'm not going to let Maxwell's wife acting a fool stop me from getting my grub on. Come on here, let's go."

Lina listened to her friend and nodded at the appropriate times. Despite her outward response, she was determined to get Maxwell back. There was no way she could let this go. She didn't know where, when, or how, but Maxwell Lee was going to get his.

Chapter Twenty-Two

"Are you going to tell me where we're going?" Lina walked through the living room of her apartment barefoot, putting an earring in.

Charles sat on the couch and watched her pace back and forth. "I want you to meet my parents. We're going over there for dinner."

Stopping mid stride, Lina turned to him and lowered her hands. "We're going where, to have dinner with who?"

Standing, Charles approached Lina and placed his hands around her waist. "You heard me." he kissed her on the neck. "I want you to meet my parents. My mother has been cooking all day. I know you don't want to disappoint my moms."

Lina eased out of his grip. "I don't know if I'm ready. Meeting your parents is a big move. What will I say? What do I do when I get there?"

"Relax, Lina. You only need to be yourself. You don't have to put on airs for anyone." Charles pulled her back into his arms and smacked her on the butt.

"Yeah, you're saying that now, but women are funny about their sons." Lina put her arms around his neck and pulled his face down to hers for a kiss.

Breaking from her embrace, Charles said, "Hurry up, woman. We need to get out of here."

"Okay, I'm hurrying." Lina skipped across the room and rushed to the bedroom. She entered the walk-in closet and searched for her strappy high heel sandals. Lina's outfit was simple. She wore a fitted light blue V-neck t-shirt with crystal stones that spelled out FAVORED on the front and denim capris. She returned to find Charles playing with Sweetie.

"Is she going to be alright being here alone?" Charles asked, patting the small dog on her head.

"Yes, she'll be fine. She's already gone out, and everything she needs is where she can get to it." Lina picked up the pooch and gave her a hug. "Mommy will be back in a little bit. Be a good girl for me, Sweetie."

The couple arrived at the Davenport residence in less than twenty minutes. The tan, two-story, brick structure appeared well kept. The lush green lawn looked freshly cut. The lawn was enhanced with flowerbeds filled with colorful perennials.

Charles took Lina by the hand and led her up the wide concrete stairs to the front door. He pressed the doorbell and waited for his parents to answer. Pulling Lina's hand up to his lips, he kissed the back of her hand and then her cheek.

A woman appeared at the door with smooth mocha skin. Her silver hair was pulled into a neat bun. Extending her arms, she pulled Charles in for a hug. "Come here, Charlie, and give your mama a hug." Mrs. Davenport turned her attention to Lina. "You must be Lina. I've heard so much about you. Charlie didn't tell me you were so beautiful." She stretched her arms out once again and enveloped Lina in an embrace. "Well, don't stand out here in this heat. Come on in the house." Mrs. Davenport took Lina by the hand and led her inside with Charles following close behind.

Everyone entered the living room where they found a man that looked like an older version of Charles sitting in a large plush chair. The man stood and walked over to meet them. He gave Charles a handshake followed by a hug.

"How you doing, son? It's good to see you." The senior Mr. Davenport looked over at Lina. "How are you, young lady?"

"I'm good. Thank you for asking." Lina extended her hand to Mr. Davenport.

Disregarding her hand, he pulled her in for a hug. "We don't shake hands around here, especially when you're family. We're hugging folk."

"Yes, sir," Lina said with a smile.

"Mama, you got it smelling good in here. What did you cook?"

"Nothing much. I put on a pot roast, some potatoes, corn on the cob and collard greens. Of course, your daddy wasn't satisfied until I fixed a sweet potato pie. Everything is ready if you all want to go and get cleaned up. I'll go ahead and set the food on the table."

"Please let me help you with that," Lina offered. "I just need to wash my hands first."

Mrs. Davenport looked at Lina with a wide grin. "Thank you, Lina. I appreciate your help. Son, will you show her where the powder room is."

Charles escorted Lina down the hall to a small restroom. The room housed a commode and white pedestal sink. She washed her hands and quickly made her way to the dining room where Mrs. Davenport was waiting for her. Mrs.

Davenport had already placed the food in serving dishes and put them on the table. The only thing left to do was to add the plates, utensils, and glasses.

Lina admired the antique oak dining table with a matching buffet and China cabinet. A stack of plates sat on the buffet, along with silverware and crystal goblets. Mrs. Davenport had even gone to the trouble of filling the ice bucket. Lina set the plates on the table. She neatly folded cloth napkins and laid them beside the plates, topping the napkins with the silverware. Lastly, she placed the goblets on the table and filled each goblet with ice and fruit punch before taking a seat.

"Thank you so much for your help, Lina," Mrs. Davenport said before taking her seat at the table. "Honey, will you do us the honors?" she asked her husband, extending her hands to Charles and Lina."

"Of course. Please bow your heads." Everyone complied and Mr. Davenport prayed a blessing over their meal. "Heavenly Father, we thank You for this day and for all of the blessings You have bestowed upon us. Now, Father, I ask that You bless this meal for the nourishment of our bodies to give strength. Bless the precious hands that prepared it, and, Father, we ask that You look on those who don't have. Bless them as only You can. In Your Son Jesus' name, Amen. Let's eat."

The sound of clanking dishes filled the room as each person filled their plates. Lina dug her fork into the pot roast and devoured a bite of the succulent meat. "Ummm, this is delicious. Mrs. Davenport you're taking my mind straight to Durham right now." She scooped a forkful of potatoes and added a piece of roast on the end before taking her next bite.

"I'm glad you're enjoying it." Mrs. Davenport beamed with pride. "You mentioned Durham. Are you originally from North Carolina?"

"Yes, ma'am. Born and raised. That's where all of my family is."

"Is that so?" Mr. Davenport interjected. "I have an aunt in Durham. She's my mother's only surviving sibling. We try to get down there to visit her at least once a year."

"What brought you to Chicago?" Mrs. Davenport asked. The doorbell rang before Lina could answer. "Now who could be popping up right when we've sat down to dinner?" She placed her napkin on the table and pushed her chair back.

"Mom, I'll get it," Charles offered, rising from the table.

"No, you stay here I'll get it." Mrs. Davenport left the table and returned with a scantily clad woman.

"Hey, Daddy," she said, walking around the table and hugging Mr. Davenport. "What's up, big bruh?" she said to Charles, pinching him on the cheek. "And who do we have here?" she asked, turning to Lina. She looked Lina up and down as if she were sizing her up.

"This is my girlfriend, Lina. Lina, this is my baby sister, Kellis."

Lina wiped her mouth with her napkin. "It's nice to meet you, Kellis."

"Umm hmmm. Nice to meet you too."

"Go get cleaned up and come on back here to get something to eat, Kellis. I swear you're nothing but skin and bones. Next time you come up in here make sure you put on some more clothes. You know better than to show up wearing a halter top and miniskirt. It may be summertime but it is not hot enough for all of that."

Kellis let out an audible sigh and rolled her eyes. Despite her nonverbal defiance she complied with her mother's wishes. Moments later she returned to the table. She'd added a T-shirt to her outfit to pacify her mother. "Is this better?" Kellis asked, extending her arms and taking a bow.

"Girl, sit your behind down and stop being silly." Mrs. Davenport couldn't help but to laugh at her daughter's antics.

Grabbing a plate and utensils from the buffet, Kellis pulled out the chair next to her brother and took a seat. She filled her plate with the delectable offerings until there was no empty space left. "Will you pass me one of those?" She asked Lina, pointing to the basket of cornbread muffins sitting on the table between Lina and Mr. Davenport.

"Mama, you threw down on this," Kellis complimented. She attacked her plate like she hadn't eaten in weeks.

"Dang, girl, slowdown. We all have our own plate. Nobody's going to take yours," Charles teased.

"Shut up, Charlie. I'm hungry and this food is good. How about you worry about your own self." Kellis resumed eating as if her brother had never interrupted her. "So, how long have y'all been together?" she asked between bites, looking back and forth between Charles and Lina.

"About a month," Lina answered.

"Wow, Charlie, you're moving fast. You ain't never brought a woman to dinner after only dating a month."

"Not that it's any of your business, but Lina and I have known each other for years. We used to work together."

"Lina, Lina," Kellis repeated the name as if she were trying to recall where she'd heard it before. "Oh, I thought your name sounded familiar. You're the photographer Charlie used to go on all those trips with. I remember him mentioning you. I thought y'all would've been together as much as he talked about you."

"Kellis, eat your food and stop embarrassing your brother," Mrs. Davenport interjected.

Lina looked at Charles and smiled. She could see the look of embarrassment he was trying to cover up. She felt bad for him but at the same time she was glad it was him and not her. Lina could only imagine the embarrassment she would feel if Charles were to have dinner with her family. Between her brother and three sisters, not to mention her cousin, there's no telling what would be said.

Kellis pushed her plate aside and took a gulp of fruit punch. She held the glass in her hand and shook the liquid around, clanking the ice cubes together. "So, Lina. Do you take pictures of regular people, or just celebrities and stuff?"

"I don't limit myself to celebrities. I photograph all types of people and objects as well." Lina had adjusted to Kellis' personality and endured her inquisition without offence.

"I've been saying I want to get some real pictures done. All my pictures are taken with a cell phone. I've always wondered what it would be like to have a real photo shoot. I think that would be dope."

"You've never said anything to me about wanting to have a photoshoot. I could have easily arranged one," Charles said.

"She needs to get some decent clothes before she thinks about having a photoshoot. With the way Kellis has been dressing since she hooked up with that boy, what's his name, Bo, or something." She poked her lips out, "I'm sure that's not what his mama named him. Anyway after she started messing around with him she's been dressing like somebody straight off the street."

"Mom," Charles said with pleading eyes darting from his mother to his sister.

"Baby, leave this girl alone. You've been picking on her from the moment she got here." He reached out and rubbed Kellis on the arm. "I'm glad she's here. It doesn't matter what she's wearing. At least she's here."

For the first time, Mrs. Davenport saw the hurt in her daughter's eyes.

"Come on, Charlie. Let's knock these dishes out," Kellis said, pushing back from the table.

"I'll be glad to help," Lina offered.

"Nah, that's okay. Me and Charlie have a routine. There's a certain way we do the dishes which helps us to get done super fast."

"Oh, okay," Lina replied.

"Baby, why don't you help me clear the table," Charles said, directing his attention to Lina. He smiled, giving her the look he knew would make her melt. In his own way, he was letting her know she was important to him and would never be excluded.

Chapter Twenty-Three

Lina was happy to be back in the comfort of her own home. Dinner with the Davenports had turned out better than she expected. Charles' sister was a bit over the top in her opinion but it was nothing Lina couldn't handle. Although she hadn't had many relationships, Lina knew serious relationships always included the couple and their families. Every family had issues and it would take true love to overcome them.

Taking a seat next to Lina on the couch, Charles pulled her into his arms. Sweetie, climbed on the couch next to Lina. "We overcame a big hurdle today. My mom likes you a lot. She's already texting me asking when we'll be back."

"Your parents are sweet. I enjoyed being over there. Kellis is a trip," Lina said, chuckling.

"Yeah, you have to overlook my little sister. She's a wildcard. We never know what she's going to do or say. She means well though."

"I like her. Kellis came across as authentic. I can deal with someone like her. With a person like Kellis you don't have to wonder where you stand. She's straight up with you, which is better than someone who is one way in your presence and totally different behind your back."

"You make a good point. I just know my sister and I see her potential. Her mouth and actions lately have closed more doors for her than anything."

"Besides the obvious, the two of you seem like complete opposites." Lina was curious about the relationship with Kellis and the Davenports, but she didn't want to press too much. She figured she would show interest but allow Charles to lead the conversation.

Charles stared out at nothing in particular. He looked to be deep in thought. Lina rubbed his thigh and kissed his cheek before rising. "I'm going to grab something to drink. Do you want anything?"

"No, I'm fine." Charles got up and followed Lina into the kitchen. "On second thought, I'll take a bottle of Coke if you have any."

"I sure do." Lina started making the sugary carbonated beverage a part of her grocery list after she and Charles officially started dating. Although he liked her iced tea, he preferred carbonated beverages. Lina wanted to make sure when Charles was with her he didn't want for anything. Reaching into the fridge, Lina grabbed the bottle of Coke and handed it to Charles.

"Thank you," he said before opening the bottle and taking a gulp. "Ahh, that's a good one." He followed Lina back into the living room and plopped down in front of the TV. "Kellis hasn't always been like this."

Lina could tell the issue with his sister was weighing heavy on Charles because he kept bring her up. She decided to hear him out. "Oh, what changed?"

"My sister was in school, doing good. She was a year away from getting her bachelor's degree in education. She hooked up with this dude from the neighborhood. Everybody knows him. We also know he's up to no good. Apparently, Kellis became involved with him last summer when she was home from school. He's in the game and my sister got caught up in his fast-talking and dirty money. My parents have always provided a good life for us. Kellis knew whatever our parents couldn't do for her, I was willing to take up the slack. None of that means anything when you have a man offering to let you use money as toilet paper. I never thought my little sister would fall for that trap."

"I'm sure you tried to talk to her. Why didn't she listen to you?"

"Probably the same reason you didn't listen to your family when they tried to talk you out of moving away. She wanted to run her own life and she felt our input was interfering with her decisions."

Lina shifted in her seat and leaned forward so she was no longer snuggled in Charles' arm. "Surely, you're not comparing my decision to move here to further my career, to Kellis' decision to quit school and become involved with that guy."

"No, baby, I'm not implying that at all. I'm referring to the desire to make your own decisions. My parents were strict on Kellis growing up. I have to admit, so was I. She even went as far as to tell me I made her feel like she had three parents instead of a sibling. What good big brother do you know who won't look out for their younger siblings. Besides, she felt mom and dad were strict, but compared to me Kellis got away with a bunch of stuff. I love my sister, so naturally I wanted to protect her. I keep praying for her and hoping one day she'll come back to what she knows is right."

Settling back into Charles' arms, Lina said, "Praying for her and being there for her when she needs you is the best thing you can do. Eventually she'll come around. She obviously loves you and your parents. It'll all work out."

Charles wrapped his arms around Lina and hugged her tight. "You know you're next right?" he asked, kissing her on top of her head.

"Next for what?"

"The parents. Let's go to Durham. I want to meet your family. I'm traveling to Raleigh soon for a conference. I know you miss your family and I'm sure they miss you. I think it would be great if you went with me. It'll give you the opportunity to spend some time at home and me a chance to meet your family."

"What if I'm not ready for you to meet my family?" Lina asked, folding her arms.

"Are you serious? I thought we were doing good."

"We *are* doing good. I just know my interaction with Kellis is going to feel like a walk in the park compared to how my family is going to drill you. You know I'm the baby and they are all protective of me. Besides, there's a lot more of them than there is of your family. I'm not trying to put my man in front of the firing squad."

"Baby, they can throw anything they want my way, it won't bother me. I can take it. I stand up for what's mine." He kissed her lips between the words he uttered. "And, baby, you are mine." Charles pulled Lina onto his lap and planted kisses on her face and neck. "Now, call your folks and say guess who's coming to dinner."

Lina burst into laughter. "You are so cheesy, but that's okay, I love you anyway."

"I love you too, sweetheart." Charles turned Lina's face toward his. "Baby, I really need you to be with me on this. It's important."

Lina shook her head in frustration. She didn't want to

be forced into a decision. The more she pondered it she realized there was no real reason to deny his request. He'd made some valid points. Her mother had been requesting she come for a visit. The only person she'd told about her relationship with Charles was her sister, Zarion. Zarion threatened to make a trip to Chicago so she could meet the man who chose to love her sister despite her illness.

"When are you planning to take the trip?" Lina asked, hoping it was several weeks away.

"Next week. The conference is scheduled for Wednesday, Thursday, and Friday. I can extend the trip a couple of days and we can fly back on Sunday. Don't worry, we'll get separate hotel rooms."

"Separate rooms? You mean separate locations. You're crazy if you think I'm going to be home with my family and stay in a hotel. My mother wouldn't hear of it. What are you trying to do, get me banned from the family?"

Charles raised his palms. "My bad, I didn't think it through. I guess I took it for granted the fact I live in the same city as my parents. I'm sure my mother would be equally offended if I came home from out of town and didn't stay at her house." Kissing Lina on the shoulder, he asked in a deep, spicy tone, "So does this mean you'll go?"

"Maybe. I need to check my calendar and see if there's anything I can move around. I'll also have to see if Cheri can look after Sweetie. It would be nice to see my parents and my precious nephew. I'll bet he has gotten so big. I haven't gotten a chance to see him playing with his t-ball set I bought him yet, except on FaceTime."

"Then it's settled. I'll have my assistant make the arrangements when I get to work tomorrow. You kill me trying to act all hard. You just wanted to hear me beg didn't you?" Taking her hand, Charles rubbed gently, massaging first her palms and then each finger. Lina relaxed under his touch.

"Oh shoot," she called out. "I left my ring in your car."

"Are you sure? I don't recall seeing a ring."

"I'm pretty sure. I remember taking it off to put lotion on my hands the other night when we were going to dinner. I can't believe I haven't missed it before now. I guess you massaging my hand made me think about it."

"Baby, you must be mistaken. I cleaned my car out yesterday. I didn't see a ring," he lied. "I'll look again tomorrow when it's light out. It wouldn't do any good to check now—it's too dark outside."

"Please check for me, baby. That ring is very special to me. My daddy gave it to me. He made me promise to only replace it with my wedding ring. I certainly can't go to Durham without it." Lina was visibly upset.

"Sweetheart, calm down. We'll find the ring."

Charles felt bad about keeping secrets from Lina. It was hard seeing her upset. He'd found the ring while cleaning out his car, but if things were going to work out the way he planned he had to keep quiet.

Chapter Twenty-Four

"It's so pretty outside today. I don't know why I let you talk me into coming to this old funky gym. We could have walked outside and enjoyed the fresh breeze and changing scenery." Cheri complained. She hated going to the gym and always made a point of letting Lina know.

"Stop complaining. Cheri. You do this every time we come here." Lina stood to the side of the treadmill and adjusted the settings. She hopped onto the slow moving belt to catch her stride. "When we finish our workout you're always glad we came so you may as well save your whining." Lina reached over and increased the speed on Cheri's machine.

"Stop touching my machine, Lina." Cheri pressed the button, bringing the speed back down. "Just because you like to work out like you're training for the Olympics doesn't mean I do."

Lina laughed as her pace quickened to a jog. "Running is so exhilarating. Come on, Cheri, pick it up." She reached over to Cheri's machine only to have her friend smack her hand.

"Say what you want, I know you too well to fall for your crap. You only get like this when something is weighing heavy on your mind. What's up, buttercup?"

"Nothing, I'm good."

"And I'm great. Now tell me the truth. Is there something going on with you and Charles?"

Lina reduced the speed on the machine, slowing her pace. Cheri was right, she could never hide anything from her. "Girl, he wants to go to Durham."

"Durham, for what?" Cheri stopped her machine and snapped her head in Lina's direction, realizing what her friend said. "Oh, he wants to go to Durham. Your family's in Durham."

"Duh, Cheri."

"He wants to meet your family? Wow, Lina, that's big. Didn't you meet his family a few days ago and now he wants to meet yours?" Cheri picked up her towel and wiped imaginary sweat from her forehead. "What did you say?"

"What could I say? It's not like I could tell him no, especially after we had just left his parents' house."

"By the way, how did meeting his parents go? I feel like we haven't talked in forever."

Lina continued her walk, prompting Cheri to start her machine up again. "His parents are cool. I enjoyed myself and I could tell they like me. His sister on the other hand is a trip. She is totally opposite from Charles. She tried to come for me, but you know me. I can hold my own."

"Yeah, she probably didn't realize you were cray cray."

Shut up, Cheri," Lina said, laughing. "Things smoothed out pretty quick. She calmed down when she saw I wasn't intimidated by her. She even had the nerve to try and exclude me from helping with the dishes when I offered, talking about her and Charles could handle it. Girl, my boo was like come on, baby."

"Okay, okay, he let her know where he stood when it

comes to you. Good job, Charles. See, that's how we're different. I would have offered to help clean out of courtesy, but as soon as I heard a no, I would have ran my butt to the family room or somewhere and sat down."

"Girl, you're a mess."

"I'm just telling the truth," Cheri said while turning her treadmill off once again. She turned her body toward Lina. "I'm confused. How did going to Durham come up? I mean was he like, okay since you met my family now I need to meet yours? Come on, girl. I need details."

"Not really. When we got back to my apartment we talked about his sister for a little bit. Girl, I won't lie, I kinda felt sorry for her. Their mama was so hard on her. Mind you, she did come in the house looking a little ratchet. She's thin as a rail with a little pudgy stomach, but homegirl was wearing a halter top and miniskirt."

"She ain't no 3-0-4 is she?" Cheri asked, giving the street acronym for whore.

"No! At least I don't think so. Charles said she has a boyfriend. From the way he described the guy it sounds like he may be a drug dealer." Lina pressed the cool down button on her machine, slowing her pace. "Anyway, their mom talked about her from the time she got there until their father stepped in. I could see in her eyes she was hurt. I mean, the stuff their mom was saying is not stuff you should bring up or say in front of company."

"Maybe his mom felt like you weren't company. Maybe she saw you as family."

"Even still, it was my first time meeting them. It wasn't cool."

"Okay, now back to Durham," Cheri said in an attempt to bring Lina back to the subject at hand. She loved Lina, but she knew her friend could easily get sidetracked.

"Yeah, so when we made it back to my apartment, Charles said I was next. Then he told me he has to go to Raleigh for a conference for work and asked if I would join him. You know Raleigh and Durham are twin cities. He said if I went with him I could go home to see my family and he could meet them."

"I can't believe you agreed to it."

"I was hesitant, but I started thinking why not. He tells me all the time how much he loves me. It's not like he's a stranger, we've known each other for years. Since we became a couple he's never given me a reason to believe his actions are insincere. I couldn't find any real reason to say no. I do need you to take care of Sweetie for me, though."

"Yeah, I'll look after Sweetie." Cheri paused taking in all Lina had shared with her. "Wow, Lina, this is big. Meeting the parents and family. That's serious. Ooh," Cheri placed her hands on her hips. "What if he's..."

Lina held her hand up. "Don't you dare say it. I refuse to let my mind go there."

Cheri smacked her lips in defiance. "We shall see."

Chapter Twenty-Five

Lina closed her eyes and braced for impact. The sound of screeching tires hitting the pavement welcomed her home to the state where she was born and raised. North Carolina offered Lina as much love as it did pain. She loved coming home to see her family, but the route to her parents' house caused her to see the clinic where she'd received the life altering HIV test results so many years ago. There was no avoiding it. Every possible route home took her past the dreaded medical facility. The building which was located at the intersection across from her parents' dead end street had been painted and the parking lot repaved, but it couldn't erase her memories. She could still picture the slot where she'd parked her car. The scent of the sterile hall leading to the doctor's office remained in her nostrils.

Charles stood and reached in the overhead compartment, removing their carryon bags. He looked at Lina and winked as he stepped aside, giving her room to exit the small space. "We're finally here, baby. Are you excited?"

Using her right index finger and thumb, Lina twirled the ring on her left hand around. "Of course, I am. Especially since I have this," she said holding up her hand, showing Charles the ring she was wearing. There was no way I was going to show up at my parents' house with you, without wearing this. My daddy would kill both of us."

"We wouldn't want that."

"No, we wouldn't." Lina and Charles shuffled behind the other passengers waiting for their opportunity to deplane. "I'm glad you found it. When you told me, you had cleaned your car out the day before, I was scared my ring had gotten sucked up in the vacuum. Thank you again, baby. You're the best."

"You're welcome, sweetheart." Charles raised the handles on their suitcases, making it easier to transport them through the terminal. He tried to appear calm before Lina, but he was a ball of nerves. Initially, he thought getting Lina to Durham was the hardest part of his plan but being there he realized it was nothing compared to the next hurdle he faced.

Lina glided through the airport, leading Charles to the baggage claim area. She was home and it showed. She behaved like a true native, moving along with no need for direction. They retrieved their bags before heading out to the shuttle for Right Way car rentals.

"Look at you, I'll bet you're glad you came now, aren't you?"

Lina turned and planted a kiss on Charles' lips. "I sure am, thank you for this."

"If bringing you to Durham is all I have to do to put a smile on your face as big as the one you're wearing, then say the word and we can come whenever your heart desires."

Pulling out from the rental car parking lot, Lina steered the Chevy Malibu onto I-40 West. Merging onto NC-147, she plunged forward. The closer she got to her parents' home, the more excited she grew. "I can't believe you didn't drive. I think this is the first time we've gone somewhere and I drove."

"Sweetheart, this is your city. The way I see it, there's no sense in me trying to figure out which way to go or listening to the robotic GPS when I can sit back, relax, and ride. You can practically get home with your eyes closed."

"Come on now, Charles. That's impossible."

"It's all how you look at it. I'll bet if I were driving and you were over here with your eyes closed, you could still give me directions that would take me straight to your parents' house."

"You may have a point there." Lina turned onto a tree-lined street and slowed the car down. She pulled into the driveway of a brick home and parked the car. "We're here," she said with a squeal.

The front door opened and Lina's mother stepped out. She extended her arms and Lina ran into her embrace.

"Mama, I missed you so much. Where's Daddy?"

"He's inside." Lydia, turned and acknowledged Charles. "Hello. How are you?" She looked him over as if she was sizing him up.

"Mama, this is Charles, my boyfriend." Lina reached out and grabbed Charles' hand. "Remember, I told you he was coming with me when I talked to you the other day."

"Chile, I was busy, I had so much going on the last time we talked I can't tell you anything you said." Lydia turned to Charles and stretched out her arms for a hug. "We're glad to have you, Charles."

Charles hugged Lydia with one arm while holding on to Lina with his other hand. "It's nice to meet you, Mrs.

Fairweather," he said, releasing the hug.

"It's nice to meet you as well. Y'all come on in here. How was your flight?" Lydia asked, leading Lina and Charles into the house.

"The flight was good. In fact, we got here a lot sooner than normal. I guess we caught a good tailwind or something," Lina answered. "Daddy," she squealed bolting toward her father.

"Hey, baby girl. How're you doing?"

"I'm good, Daddy," Lina said, giving her father a tight squeeze and kiss on his plump cheek."

"Who do we have here?" Mr. Fairweather asked, looking past Lina to Charles.

"Daddy, this is Charles, my boyfriend."

Mr. Fairweather extended his hand to Charles. "It's nice to meet you, son. Y'all have a seat."

Charles followed Lina over to the couch and took a seat. Lydia walked past the couple to the kitchen where she prepared glasses of sweet tea for the four of them. She returned carrying the tray. Jumping up from the couch, Charles grabbed the tray and placed it on the table.

Lydia grabbed a glass of tea for herself and one for her husband, Joseph, before taking a seat next to him on the loveseat. Lina followed her mother's lead and handed Charles a glass before taking one for herself.

"So, Charles, Lina tells us you're in town for a conference for work."

"Yes, that's correct. It's a three-day conference. The conference is an all day event, but we're free in the evenings."

"Oh, I see," Lydia replied, taking a sip of tea. "What is it you do, again?"

"I'm vice president of marketing for Watchman Journal."

"That sounds like a pretty important position, especially for such a young man. I'm sure your parents are quite proud of you," Mr. Fairweather said, joining the conversation.

"I'd like to think it's important. And yes, my parents are proud." Charles took a drink from his glass and returned it to the tray. He sat up straight on the couch, being careful not to appear too relaxed or too stiff.

Awkward silence fell over the room. Mr. and Mrs. Fairweather looked back and forth to Lina and Charles and then at each other. Their glances created a conversation of their own. Finally, verbalizing the unspoken conversation, Lydia asked, "Lina, where are your bags? You'll be here until Sunday, won't you? I know you're staying here, right?" Lydia fired off one question after the next.

"Yes, ma'am. My bags are in the car. I was going to have Charles bring them in before he leaves to go to the hotel later.

Satisfied with her daughter's response, Lydia nodded. "I have some chicken thawing for dinner. I'm not sure who all will make it by here since it's a Tuesday. Everybody is pretty much working. I planned a cookout for Saturday so everybody can come by and see you. I'm sure they're all looking forward to it since you don't get home often enough."

"Do you need any help fixing dinner, Mama? I've been working on my cooking skills." Lina was determined not to play into her mother's guilt trip. Lydia made the same comment every time Lina visited. Lina would usually retort but she didn't want to go back and forth with her mother in front of Charles.

Reaching out, Charles took Lina's hand and gently

squeezed. "I can assure you, Lina misses you all as much as you miss her. She talks about you guys all the time."

Lydia raised an eyebrow and looked over at her husband who was smiling. Whether he knew it or not, Charles had scored major points with the family's patriarch.

The room had grown eerily silent to the point of awkwardness. Lydia spoke up. "The chicken should be thawed by now. I better get dinner started if we're going to eat at a decent hour. Lina, come and help me." Lydia and Lina left the living room leaving Charles alone with Joseph.

Charles drummed his fingers together. He wanted to make a good impression on Lina's family, especially her parents. He recalled Lina saying her father was a sports fan. Charles was a sports fanatic. He figured he would use sports as a conversation piece.

"Mr. Fairweather, Lina tells me you're a huge sports fan. Do you follow baseball?"

"I sure do," Joseph answered, sitting up straighter on the loveseat. I'm a diehard Braves fan. What about you? I'll bet you're a Sox fan, aren't you?"

"No, sir. There aren't any real teams except the Cubs. Everybody else is just practicing."

"What you say, young buck? Somebody done told you wrong. You ain't seen the sun rise and set enough times to make a statement that crazy."

"With all due respect, Atlanta is a good team but they don't have anything on the Cubs. Atlanta is a close second. I'll give you that."

Joseph got up from his seat and snatched the television remote off the mantle. "I don't know where you got your information from, but it's wrong, dead wrong." Joseph switched on the television and pulled up the sports package where he could watch on-demand games. "Look here, let me show you what a real team looks like." He found a Braves game and tuned in. The men relaxed and enjoyed the game while Lina and her mother prepared dinner.

"Grab some potatoes and onions and cut them up for me, Lina."

Lina pulled two large bowls from the cabinet. She placed one bowl on the table and filled the other with red-skinned potatoes. Grabbing a sharp knife from the wooden knife block her mother kept on the counter, Lina went to work. She hummed while she cut up the potatoes. It felt good being in her parents' home. She and her mother didn't always agree on things, but Lina was grateful to still have her.

"Charles seems like a nice man," Lydia said as she rinsed the chicken. "There's no doubt he's crazy about you. I can tell by the way he looks at you, and he was quick to defend you when I said something about you not coming home as often as I would like."

Lina stopped peeling the potatoes, turned and looked at her mother. "He's a good guy, Mama. For as long as I've known him he's always been very kind." She turned back to the task at hand. Laughing, she continued, "I had a crush on him for years. It's hard to believe we're a couple now."

Reaching into the cabinet, Lydia pulled out several bottles of seasoning. She opened each one and sprinkled it on the chicken. Turning to Lina she spoke in a low tone, making sure the men couldn't hear her. Concern was etched on her face. "What about..."

Anticipating her question, Lina said, "He knows, Mama."

Lydia turned away from the counter. "He knows about your affliction?" she asked with great surprise.

"Yes, Mama. He knows and he still wants to be with me."

Lydia washed her hands and picked up the towel to dry them. She moved over to the table and took a seat next to Lina. "How long has he known? Did you tell him?"

Not bothering to look up, Lina sliced into the potatoes, cutting them into small chunks. "I told him shortly after we started dating. I didn't want to risk him finding out from someone else and I didn't want to hide. I figured if he was for me it would show in his response." Lina shared Charles' response with her mother up until the moment he told her he loved her. She omitted the part about the three-day wait, deeming it unnecessary.

Placing her arm around Lina's shoulder, Lydia pressed her cheek against her daughter's. "I'm so happy for you, baby. You deserve a good man, someone that's going to love you unconditionally."

The ladies heard shouting in the living room. They looked at each other with horrified expressions. Scrambling to their feet, they ran in the direction of the commotion.

"Go, man!" Mr. Fairweather yelled.

"What are you doing? Stop him!" Charles yelled in response.

When Lina and Lydia made it to the living room, they found Charles and Joseph both up on their feet yelling at the television. The ladies looked at each other in shock. They turned and headed back to the kitchen without uttering a word to the men.

Returning her focus to cooking, Lydia placed the Dutch oven on the stove and lit the fire beneath it. She added oil to the pot and waited for it to heat. "Lina, it looks like Charles gets as involved in a game as your father. I'm telling you now, if that's the case, you better make sure you have a hobby because when a game is on your father disconnects. Are you sure this is what you want?"

Chapter Twenty-Six

Charles stretched across the bed in his hotel room and reflected on his visit with Lina's parents. Things had gone well and he was grateful. It was nice to find common ground with her father. Sharing a love for sports was a major plus for him. He knew the subject of sports would always be an automatic conversation starter.

Placing his hands behind his head, Charles looked up at the ceiling. He had no doubt in his mind he loved Lina. He wasn't big on making hasty decisions but with Lina everything felt right. He wanted to move forward, however for him timing was everything. *How can I get this done?* The question hunted his inner being. Surrendering, Charles closed his eyes and said aloud, "If it's meant to be, it'll all work out."

The clock on the nightstand displayed 10:08 PM. Charles laid in bed thinking about Lina wishing she was lying next to him. Although they had never slept together he was used to being in her presence late into the night. He respected her parents' home, leaving at 9:30. Charles smiled with delight when her mother handed him a foam container filled with leftover chicken and potatoes.

Thinking back on previous trips he and Lina had taken together Charles realized this was the first time they hadn't stayed in the same location. On work related trips, their rooms were always located at the same hotel. Many times they were on the same floor. It was common for them to meet in the hotel bar for a midnight snack. Knowing Lina was so close, yet inaccessible, placed a yearning in his heart for her.

Charles reached for the remote but stopped upon hearing his phone ring. He pressed the button to answer. "Hey, sweetheart, I was just thinking of you."

"You were?" Lina replied in a teasing tone. "What were you thinking?"

"I was thinking about how much I wish you were laying here with me," he answered honestly. "Tomorrow can't get here quick enough. I'm hoping they don't keep us in this conference all day, I want to spend as much time with you as possible."

"Actually, I'm not sure we'll get together tomorrow. That's one of the reasons I was calling," Lina said. "I made plans to go shopping with my mother and sisters tomorrow evening. I'm not sure how long we'll be out. I can call you tomorrow when I know more. Or maybe I'll stop by the hotel and hang out with you for a little while tomorrow night."

"Sweetheart, you don't have to do that. The reason you came on this trip was to spend time with your family. I won't interfere with your plans. I'm sure there will be somebody at the conference I know. I'll hang out with them or just chill. Either way I'll be fine."

"Thanks, Charles."

"What about your dad? Is he going with you all?"

Lina laughed hard as if Charles had said the funniest thing she'd ever heard. "My daddy, go shopping? Never. He'll be here at the house the same as always. You can come by and hang out with him if you want. I'm sure there will be some game on you two can watch together."

"No, baby, it's alright. I was just curious." Charles and Lina continued to talk for the next thirty minutes. As much as he would have enjoyed being in her presence, he was glad she had called. Without knowing, she'd told him exactly what he needed to hear. His prayer had been answered.

Charles followed the turn-by-turn instructions given by the navigation system. Arriving at the house, he noticed the pearl Buick Enclave belonging to Lina's mother was missing from the driveway. A midnight blue Nissan Maxima with a *baby on board* decal on the back sat in its place. He figured it must have been Lina's sister, Zarion's car. Parking his rental car on the street, he got out and walked up to the door.

His heartbeat quickened with each step he took. He was sure of the decision he'd made but uncertain of the response he would get. The sound of the television playing inside led him to believe there was someone home. Charles knocked on the door and waited for a response.

"Who is it?" Joseph called out from inside.

The sound was muffled like he was far away but Charles responded anyway. "It's Charles."

"Who'd you say?" Joseph asked again, this time sounding closer to the door.

"It's Charles, Lina's boyfriend."

Joseph opened the door with a smile. "Hey, Charles, man. How're you doing?"

"I'm doing good." He waited for Mr. Fairweather to step aside to allow him to enter but he didn't.

"Lina's not here. They're out shopping. They'll probably be gone until the mall closes. I'd invite you in, but I doubt you'd want to wait that long. I know I wouldn't."

"Actually, I came by to talk to you if you have time. I knew Lina would be gone and thought maybe this would be a good time."

"Oh," Joseph replied, widening his eyes. "Come on in," he said, stepping aside. "Can I offer you something to drink or a snack?" he asked, walking toward the couch.

"No, I'm fine. Thank you."

"Okay, have a seat. What's on your mind?"

Charles swallowed hard, forcing the lump in his throat back down. "Mr. Fairweather, I've known Lina for quite some time now. I'm not sure if you're aware, we started out working together. We went on a lot of trips for work related projects. It was during those trips I was afforded the opportunity to truly get to know her." Charles paused to gauge Joseph's reaction "Being in the positions we were in I was unable to pursue her romantically. As fate would have it, situations changed and what was once an obstacle no longer is."

Clearing his throat, Charles loosened the tie he was still wearing. "Lina and I have been seeing each other exclusively for a couple months. I know that may seem like a short time but we've had years to get to know one another." Charles readjusted himself on the couch and rubbed his hand on his thighs. "Mr. Fairweather, I'm in love with your daughter. I can't imagine my life without her and there's no other woman I want besides her. I'm here to ask you for Lina's hand in marriage."

Joseph sat on the edge of his chair and leaned forward. "Son, are you sure about this? Taking on a wife is a big responsibility. With Lina, well..." Joseph's words trailed off.

"I know about her condition and I still want to be with her. I've done some research and with the treatments available now, there's no reason why we can't have a full life together."

Joseph shook his head. "You're saying this now, but how do I know you won't run at the first sight of trouble?"

"With all due respect, Mr. Fairweather, when Lina told me about her condition I had the opportunity then to walk away. I chose to stay because I love her. If you would do me the honor of allowing me her hand, I'd be forever grateful. I'll continue to love her, and I will provide for her. My parents have been married over thirty-five years so I know what it takes to keep it together."

Joseph rose from his seat and walked over to Charles who also stood. He extended his hand for a handshake, before pulling him in for a hug. Patting Charles on the back, Joseph said, "I'd be honored to give you my daughter's hand."

Chapter Twenty-Seven

Music played through the speakers, mingled with laughter and conversation. The cookout was in full swing in the backyard of the Fairweather's home. The smell of barbecue filled the air, sending the neighborhood dogs into a barking frenzy. A tent had been set up with tables and chairs along with a eight foot long table for the food. Lina and her sisters walked out of the house in a single file line carrying aluminum pans filled with baked beans, potato salad, and spaghetti. They placed the dishes on the table next to a stack of disposable plates, utensils, napkins, and a pile of buns.

Charles, Gerald, and Zarion's husband stood around the grill chatting with Mr. Fairweather as he prepared the meat.

Lina and Charles shared stolen glances while she and her sisters helped prepare the food. The joy she felt, having him around was inexplicable. Her family took to him right away treating him as if he was a permanent fixture. Lina watched in delight as her nephew Daniel approached Charles who readily picked him up. He held him in his arms on his belly with the little boys arms outstretched in front of him. Charles turned in circles giving Daniel the illusion of flying like he was superman. Daniel exploded in laughter. Thoughts of Charles as a father invaded Lina's mind.

Followed by a looming sadness she forced back. She was determined not to allow her condition to interfere with the family's fun.

"Bring me the big roaster pan so I can get this meat off the grill," Mr. Fairweather called out to no one in particular.

"I'll get it, Daddy," Lina replied, heading into the house.

Charles followed her immediately. He watched as Lina went into the pantry and fumbled through the large pots and pans. She spotted the roaster located on a high shelf. Lina reached above her head for the pan, but soon discovered she wasn't tall enough. Reaching over her, Charles grabbed the pan.

"Watch out, baby. I got it," he said, kissing her on the cheek.

"I could've gotten it," Lina said, crossing her arms and poking out her lips.

"I know you could have, baby, but you don't have to. That's what I'm here for."

"Alright, Mr. strongman. Bring it over here so I can rinse it out," she said, standing by the sink.

Charles complied. When she was finished, he grabbed the pan and followed her back outside. When they made it to the yard, everyone was staring at them.

"What?" Lina asked with a raised eyebrow.

"Don't be looking at us all crazy. Y'all the ones who took ten minutes to get a pan," Zarion teased. "What were y'all in there doing?"

"We weren't doing anything. I had to find the pan and then rinse it out." Lina tilted her head and turned up her lip as if she had just considered what her sister said. "We were not gone ten minutes. Y'all ought to be ashamed of yourselves."

The crowd burst into laughter. They enjoyed teasing Lina about her relationship. Seeing her happy with Charles brought them all joy.

"Bring me that pan before this meat burns," Mr. Fairweather called out.

Everyone sat around eating and talking. The combination of conversation and laughter harmonized like music throughout the tent. Charles looked over at Lina's father and gave a slight nod. Joseph replied by raising his chin. They made subtle movements so the others wouldn't know what was going on.

"The food was delicious," Charles said, patting his stomach. "I don't know how, but I still feel empty."

Lina looked at him and then over at the table where the food had been set up buffet style. "Baby, get up and get what you want. There's plenty left. No one here will mind."

Kissing Lina on the cheek, he replied, "I believe I'll do just that." Charles stood and pushed his chair back from the table. Instead of heading to the table, he dropped down on one knee behind Lina.

Busy talking to her sister, Javonne, Lina didn't notice what was happening until her mother gasped and said, "Oh my God."

Lina turned to see what was going on and found Charles kneeling with an open ring box. The three-carat diamond solitaire sparkled despite the shade of the tent. Instant tears formed in Lina's eyes. A hush fell over the tent when Charles started to speak.

"From the moment I first laid eyes on you, I knew there was something different about you. When we were blessed with the opportunity to travel together our bond grew stronger. I was able to get to know you on a deeper, more meaningful, level. Given the positon we were in, I didn't know how we could move forward so I prayed about it and God opened a door that allowed us to be together. Lina, you are an incredible woman. I love you with all that's in me. I can't imagine my life without you in it. I want you to know my love for you is real. If you'll do me the honor of becoming my wife, I will love you like you've never been loved before."

Reaching out with his free hand, he pulled Lina up from her seat. "Sweetheart, say you'll make me the happiest man alive. Lina Fairweather, will you marry me?"

Fresh tears poured from Lina's eyes. She nodded her head slowly then more rapid. "Yes, Charles, I'll marry you, baby. Yes."

Charles stood and pulled Lina into his arms. He kissed her passionately inciting oohs and ahhs from her family. Releasing her, Charles turned to Joseph. He lifted Lina's left hand and placed his hand on the ring her father had placed there so many years ago. "Mr. Fairweather, with your permission, I'd like to replace your ring with mine."

"Go 'head, son. I know you'll take care of my baby."

Pulling gently on the ring, Charles slipped it off Lina's hand and replaced it with the diamond engagement ring. He placed her father's ring on her right hand.

Lydia jumped up and ran over to her youngest daughter, pulling her and Charles into a group hug. She studied Lina's ring. "Ooh wee, baby. Look at this ring. Y'all turn on some music. This cookout has turned into an engagement party. My baby is getting married."

In no time the family was up on their feet congratulating

the couple. The women pulled Lina to one side, examining her ring and talking about wedding ideas while the men congregated with congratulatory pats on Charles' back.

At the end of the cookout, Charles and Lina excused themselves. Although they enjoyed spending time with Lina's family, they hadn't had the opportunity to talk since Lina accepted the marriage proposal. They decided to go for a drive to have some alone time. Once they were in the car, Charles dialed his parents. His mother answered the phone with great anticipation.

"Hey, Charlie. How did it go?"

"Hey, Mom. Where's Dad? Is he there with you?" Charles replied, without answering the question.

"Yeah, he's right here. Hold on a second. I'll put the phone on speaker." There was a brief pause before Mrs. Davenport returned to the phone. "Okay, go ahead. We're both listening."

"Hey there, son. How's it going down there in Durham?"

"Everything is going great."

"Stop stalling," Mrs. Davenport said, cutting into the conversation. "Is Lina there with you?"

"Yes, Mom, she's here. Baby, say hello to your future in-laws. She said yes!"

"Oh, my God!" Mrs. Davenport yelled into the phone. "Congratulations, you two."

"Congratulations," Mr. Davenport chimed in.

"Tell me all about it. What did you say? Where did you do it? I want details, Charlie." Mrs. Davenport was shooting off questions like fireworks.

"I know you want details, Mom, and I promise I'll fill you in, just not right now. Tell you what, Lina and I will be back home tomorrow. We'll come over and share everything with you in person."

Mrs. Davenport started to protest but relented. "I guess I can wait until tomorrow. I would rather hear everything face to face as opposed to over the phone anyway. Me and your dad will be here waiting. Welcome to the family, Lina."

"Thank you, Mrs. Davenport."

"You're going to have to cut that Mrs. Davenport stuff out. You're family now. You can call me Mom."

"Yes, ma'am," Lina replied without adding the title. They ended the call and continued their drive.

"You planned this all along, didn't you," Lina said to Charles as more of a statement than a question. "Is this why you wanted me to come on this trip with you?"

Charles grabbed her hand and kissed the back. "Sweetheart, I've known from the first time I laid eyes on you I wanted you to be my wife. I'll admit I've been thinking about this for a while. I knew I wanted your family to be involved but I didn't know how I would be able to pull it off. When I received word about the conference being here, I knew it was meant to be."

"I'm so happy, baby. I mean, really, you surprised me. I know you said you love me, and you've been so good to me, but I never expected this. Being able to share it with my family was amazing. These are the people who know everything about me. They've seen my highs and my lows. None of us ever thought this would happen for me. I don't want a long engagement. I want to become your wife as soon as possible." Lina leaned over and wrapped her arms around Charles. She kissed his cheek then his ear and neck.

"Girl, you better stop it. Otherwise, I'm going to have some explaining to do."

Lina pressed her back against the seat and crossed

her legs. She intertwined her fingers with Charles'. "Don't worry, we won't have to hold back much longer. I'm going to be yours in every way."

Chapter Twenty-Eight

Lina sat on the edge of the bed and stared at her engagement ring. This was the first opportunity she'd had to be alone. Although she knew the day was real, in her heart and mind it felt like a fairytale. The shock that registered on her face upon seeing Charles on bended knee was genuine. She accepted the proposal right away, but now she was wondering if she'd made the right decision. Charles was a young, handsome, healthy man. To marry him would be denying him the chance to father children of his own.

Reaching into her side table drawer, she pulled out the Bible she'd received from her mother following her diagnosis. At the time, Lina didn't want anything relating to her illness, even if it was a Bible. She viewed the gift as nothing more than a cruel reminder of her mistakes. From the moment she'd tossed the Bible into the drawer, she hadn't pulled it out, until now.

Running her hand over the embossed inscription, Lina read the words her mother desperately wanted her to embrace. *Trust in the Lord with all your heart.* Although the remaining words to Proverbs three and five were not engraved she finished the scripture aloud. "...and lean not on your own understanding." Lina gripped the Bible with both hands. She looked up and said, "Lord, what is it you're trying to tell me?"

Closing her eyes, Lina took both thumbs and parted the pages of the Bible. She opened her eyes to view the scriptures where the book had fallen open. A highlighted passage immediately captured her attention. *For my thoughts are not your thoughts, neither are your ways my ways, declares the Lord.* She studied the scripture found in Isaiah chapter fifty-five verse eight. Initially, she tried to rationalize the reason she was reading that particular scripture. She figured her mother had to have highlighted it at some point because she knew she hadn't.

Tears filled Lina's eyes when she realized there was no way her mother could have known she would pick up the Bible at this moment. She also hadn't searched for the scripture; she'd allowed it to fall in a random location. Lina couldn't deny the Lord speaking to her through His word. She looked up as if she was staring directly into heaven and offered up a prayer of thanks. Once she'd finished praying, Lina grabbed her phone and called her best friend.

"Hello," Cheri answered in an upbeat tone. Lina could hear Sweetie barking in the background.

"Hey, girl. How's it going?"

"Good, the same as it was yesterday, and the day before, *and* the day before that. I swear this dog knows your ringtone." Cheri giggled. "We were all sitting up here chilling and watching TV. As soon as she heard the phone ring she was off the couch, jumping up and down in the middle of the floor, barking."

"Leave my baby alone," Lina said, pouting.

"You can come and get your baby with her spoiled behind."

"Don't worry. I'll be home tomorrow. Your house will be my first stop, trust, and believe." Lina got up from her bed and pulled her suitcase out of the closet. "I'm glad Sweetie is doing good, but she's not the reason I'm calling you. I called to tell you what Charles did today in front of my family." Lina used a tone of frustration to throw Cheri off.

"Girl, what did he do? Don't tell me I'm about to have to handle this brotha. First, you had to deal with Amirah and her drama and now Charles is trippin'. Have you even heard anything else from Maxwell or his insecure wife?"

"I haven't seen or heard from that crazy woman, or the dirty bastard she calls a husband since we saw her at the restaurant. If I never see or hear from either of them again, it won't hurt my feelings. Now back to Charles, you're definitely going to have some words for him after I tell you this." Lina paused to let the anticipation build. "Today, at the cookout, this man got in front of my family and oooh," Lina sighed heavily. She moved the phone away from her mouth and released a soft giggle.

"And what, Lina? Girl, you got me up pacing the floor. I'm so mad. What'd he do?"

Lina pictured her friend pacing around the room like Madea on a Tyler Perry movie. She decided to stop toying with her friend. "Girl, this man asked me to marry him and I said yes. We're engaged."

"What!" Cheri let out a loud yelp. Sweetie barked in response. "Oh, my God, Lina. Congratulations, bestie. I knew it! I knew Charles was going to propose. I tried to tell you when we were at the gym but you weren't trying to hear it. I'm so happy for you. Even though you had me going and done raised my blood pressure, this makes up for it."

Lina filled her friend in on the details of her engagement.

Cheri immediately went into wedding mode, asking about, dates, colors, and location. Lina halted her friend's rambling by telling her she had not reached the planning stages yet. Hearing Cheri's excitement caused Lina to explode with joy once again. Lina ended the call with a promise Cheri's home would be their first stop when they arrived back in Chicago.

Charles walked around his hotel room, gathering his belongings. Their flight was leaving early the following morning. Lina's parents offered to bring her to the hotel rather than have him pick her up in Durham only to return to Raleigh to the airport. Charles wanted to protest but he knew it was the most logical decision.

Once he was all packed, he grabbed his cell phone off the table and sent separate text messages to his sister and his aunt, India. The messages contained a picture of an engagement ring with the caption I asked and she said yes. He followed it up with a selfie of him and Lina. She was holding her hand up with her fingers spread, displaying the ring. Holding on to the phone, Charles wondered which would be the first to call. Seconds later his phone vibrated in his hand.

"You have got to be kidding me. Is this for real?" Kellis started talking before Charles had the chance to say hello.

"A simple, *congratulations Charles* will suffice, Kellis."

"How am I supposed to congratulate what I don't understand, Charlie? You and her haven't even been together long. You don't think you're moving too fast?"

"No, I don't. I'm capable of making decisions for my life. It's not as if I need to explain anything to you, but I love Lina and she's the woman I want. Now stop with the jealous little sister act and congratulate me."

"I mean, if this is what you want, I'm all for it. I know you know what you're doing. I won't stand in your way. Just make sure you tell me congratulations when it's my turn."

"I will as long as it ain't with..."

"Don't start, Charlie," Kellis said, cutting him off. "Are you still out of town?" she asked, changing the subject.

"Yeah, I'll be home tomorrow."

"Okay then, I'll talk to you when you get home 'cause what I have to say needs to be said face to face. Bye, Charlie."

Charles shook his head. His sister was a force to be reckoned with but he loved her and nothing she said or did would ever change that. He tossed his phone on the cushion next to him and flipped on the TV. The sound of a bell drew his attention to his phone. The tone notified him of an incoming text message. A smiling emoji with hearts in the place of eyes and confetti filled his screen. A second message with the words Congratulations, I want to meet her, immediately followed the first text.

Thanks will do. Charles texted back. "Ah, man," he said aloud, placing his hand on his forehead. The thought had just occurred to him he shared Lina's status with India after he promised her he wouldn't tell anyone. If India said anything to Lina, his engagement would be over before it began.

Chapter Twenty-Nine

"Mother, I don't want a big wedding, and I don't want to get married in Durham." Lina rolled her eyes as she held the phone up to her ear. Lydia had made a point to call her every day since she and Charles returned to Chicago. Every conversation centered around Lina's upcoming nuptials.

"You are the youngest child. Why don't you want a big wedding, Lina? Is it because of the expense? You don't have to worry about the cost. Your father and I have it under control. Even your brother and sisters are willing to chip in to make your day as special as possible. Why are you being so difficult, child?" Lydia huffed. "Not one time in all these conversations have I heard you mention Charles. I'm sure with him being the only son, his parents want him to have a real wedding too."

"I don't want a lot of fanfare, Mama. Charles told me however I want the wedding to be, it's fine with him. We'll have an intimate ceremony here in Chicago, take a few pictures, and start our life as man and wife. Easy peasy," Lina spoke with finality. She was tired of going back and forth about the wedding.

"Speaking of Chicago," Lydia said, busting open the door Lina tried to close on their conversation, "Why on earth do you want to have the wedding in Chicago? All of your family is here in Durham. The only people in Chicago are

Charles' family and your best friend. That's all of what—six people? Whereas, there are at least fifty of us here. Everyone knows the wedding is supposed to be held in the bride's hometown. That's just plain ole wedding etiquette."

"Again, Mother, having the wedding in Chicago was my decision. I know my family is in Durham, and believe me, I love each and every one of you, but I live in Chicago. This is my home." Lina softened her tone, "Mama, you know Durham is a sore spot for me. Durham is where my life was altered forever. I know you don't like to think about it, but I live with it every single day. I don't want what is supposed to be the happiest day of my life blemished by that place."

"Lina, stop it," Lydia said in an elevated tone. For years I have listened to you whine and complain about how much you hate Durham because of your illness. Yes, you experienced something horrible you are forced to live with. When are you ever going to move on? You, too must be accountable for your choices. What Kaine did was wrong, but you were a willing participant. You can't continue to live your life looking at things one-sided. When you acknowledge your shortcomings, and take responsibility, then you can finally heal."

Lydia's tone softened. "Baby girl, I've watched you carry this burden for all these years when it was never your burden to carry. You are not alone in the battle you fight. Many people share the same affliction in their bodies. You have completely turned your heart and mind from the city of Durham when in reality Durham is not the problem. The problem is you've never allowed the Lord to heal you."

"Mama, this disease is incurable. Trust me, the moment they come up with a cure, I will be the first in line. Until then, I'm forced to deal with the fact my life will never be normal. I've made peace with it, so I don't need healing. And before you say it, I know God is a healer and miracle worker so I'm not denying that. I'm simply accepting my life as it is."

"You've proven my point, Lina. HIV is not why you need healing; it's not your issue. The healing you need is for your heart. You are full of bitterness and anger. Before Kaine died, you were able to direct your anger toward him. Now that he's gone, you direct your anger toward Durham. Baby, until you ask God to heal you completely and open yourself up to receive the healing, you will never truly be happy. You'll find something wrong in every situation because it's misplaced anger. Please don't get married with all of this built up in your heart. If you do, you'll take it into your marriage and make Charles pay for what Kaine did. When you get time, go before God and ask Him to heal your heart completely." Lydia added a few parting words of wisdom, "Don't rule out Durham for your wedding. God may want to use a joyous occasion to remove the stain of the painful situation you experienced here. Remember, good always cancels out bad. I love you."

"I love you too, Mama." Lina disconnected the call and plopped down on the couch. As hard as it was to hear her mother's words, she knew she was right. She had never asked God to heal her heart. There was no since in putting it off any longer. Heartbroken, Lina didn't have a lot of words to say. She clasped her hands together and with a sincere heart she prayed, "Lord, please heal my heart. I don't want to go another day carrying this weight. You said to cast my cares on You. Well, Lord, I'm casting and I believe You will do the rest. Thank You in advance for my healing. In Jesus' name, Amen.

Lina ended her prayer and checked the time. She had been on the phone with her mother for over an hour. Charles was due to arrive in less than fifteen minutes and she still wasn't ready. She was dressed but her hair was a different story. On their way home from Raleigh he'd mentioned his aunt India. He said he wanted them to meet because India was more like a sister to him than an aunt.

With little time to spare, Lina hurried to the bathroom and pulled her hair into a messy bun. She applied a clear gloss to her lips and put on diamond studded earrings. Stepping back from the mirror, she examined her outfit. The flowy pastel blue jumper accentuated her curves. "Something is missing," Lina said, focusing on the off the shoulder design. She snapped her fingers suddenly, remembering what she lacked. Moving into her bedroom, she rummaged through the jewelry box she received as a birthday gift from Cheri. Clasping the silver necklace with the small diamond pendant, she added a matching bracelet and her outfit was complete.

Charles arrived just as Lina dabbed perfume behind her ears. She opened the door and greeted him with a kiss.

"Sweetheart, you look gorgeous," he said, examining her outfit. Her light denim wedge sandals gave her enough height, allowing them to kiss without her having to stand on tiptoes. "Are you ready to go? I told India we would be there in about forty-five minutes. She's looking forward to meeting you. Believe me when I tell you, she has already called me at least three times today."

"I'm ready." Lina picked up her purse and keys from the table located near the door and headed out.

"I think you and India are going to get along great. The two of you have a lot in common. You're a photographer and she's an artist. Well, for her it's more of a hobby, but you get my point."

"Okay. Perhaps that will give us some talking points. It's always weird for me when I'm being introduced to someone, even in business. I feel like I'm an item waiting to be examined, or an object being studied."

Charles looked at Lina and frowned. "I would have never guessed that about you. You always seem confident meeting new people when we're together."

Lina let out a light chuckle. "In this business you learn how to fake it. I use boldness to hide how shy I am. People have no idea how nervous I am." With an audible sigh, she continued, "I'll never forget when I was waiting to be interviewed by you. I was shaking so hard on the inside. I figured Elizabeth would think I was having a seizure." Lina shook her head at the memory. "Oh, and when I met you and saw you were young, not the old man I expected, and you were fine and sexy, it was a wrap."

"I can see how I had that effect on you."

"What!" Lina burst into laughter at Charles' response. One thing was for sure, he could always make her laugh.

Lina scanned the radio as Charles cruised down Dan Ryan expressway. His phone rang and the familiar name and number popped up on his car's display. Pushing the button on the steering wheel, he answered the call. "Hello again, India."

"Hey, nephew, are you and Lina still coming? I thought you would have been here by now."

"Yes, India. We're on our way. I'm gonna need you to calm down before you scare my baby off. You're going to have her thinking I'm taking her to meet a crazy woman."

"Shut up, Charles. If she can't handle me I don't know

how in the world she can put up with you because you are way more of a handful than I am." She laughed before going back to her original question, "Where y'all at? I'm trying to figure out how much time I have to finish getting stuff together."

"We're about ten minutes out so whatever you need to do, you better hurry up. Now get off my phone, woman." Charles pressed the button on the steering wheel to end the call.

"Do you and her always go back and forth like that?" Lina asked with a smirk.

"Pretty much," he replied. "Growing up, my grandmother lived up the street from us. Mama always said India was my grandmother's menopause baby since she had her late in life. All of my other aunts and uncles were much older. Before I was born, my mother treated India more like she was her daughter instead of her sister. India was always at our house. When I came along, we were raised like brother and sister even though India didn't live with us. When Mama had Kellis she was so much younger than us, which left me and India to do everything together."

"I thought India was a lot older than you since she was calling you nephew."

"Man, she started doing that in high school when she was a senior and I was a sophomore. She got mad when I checked this dude who was trying to talk to her. I knew the punk wasn't no good, but because she was interested in him she started calling me nephew to try and act like she had some kind of power. Now, she only does it to irritate me."

India stood in the doorway, beaming, as Charles parked

the car. She caught a glimpse of Lina in the front seat and waved frantically. Lina smiled and waved back.

"Her name certainly fits because she looks like she and India Arie could be sisters," Lina whispered to Charles as if she was afraid India would hear her.

"You're not the first person who's made the comparison. India has always been a good sport about it though, saying she wished she had India Arie's money." Charles shifted the car to Park and turned off the ignition.

Lina pushed open her door before Charles could reach her. She didn't want to come across to his aunt as high maintenance. Charles gave her a confused look but didn't protest. Rather than react, he took her by the hand and approached India's front door.

"Hey, Charles," India said as if it was the first time she had spoken to him all day. She then turned to Lina and said, "You must be Lina. I've heard so much about you. It's nice to finally meet you." Wrapping her arms around Lina, she pulled her in for a warm embrace. She released her and stepped aside, ushering them into her home.

Charles recited his usual greeting. "What do you have to eat in here? I know you didn't invite us all the way out here and think you're going to get away with not feeding us."

"I haven't cooked. We can order a pizza or something. I didn't know if y'all had already eaten or what. Will pizza work for you, Lina, or are you in the mood for something else?"

Lina shrugged. "Pizza is fine with me. I'm not very hungry right now, but I'm sure I will be later."

The trio spent the next hour laughing and talking. India shared stories about Charles growing up while he cringed. Lina felt like she had known India for years. She could see why India and Charles got along so well. Unable to ignore her bladder any longer, Lina asked India where her restroom was located. India gave her directions and continued chatting with Charles.

Taking quick steps, Lina marched into the restroom. In her haste to relieve herself she knocked over a bottle of pills on India's vanity. She washed her hands and picked up the bottle. A wave of nausea swept through her when she read the name of the familiar medication. Feelings of déjà vu caused her to stumble. She placed one hand on the sink for support, while using her other hand to return the bottle to the vanity. She was shaking uncontrollably.

Lina bit back anger as thoughts of betrayal filled her mind. After taking several deep breaths, she calmed herself and returned to the living room where Charles and India were seated.

"Are you okay, sweetheart?" Charles asked, noticing Lina's flustered appearance.

"I'm fine. What did I miss?"

India looked over at Charles and then at Lina. "You didn't miss much. Your timing is perfect. I was about to ask Charles about the wedding. Have the two of you decided on a location?"

"Yeah, it's going to be in Durham," Lina answered before Charles had the opportunity to say anything.

"Durham? I thought you wanted to have it here. You said you didn't want to get married in Durham." The confusion he felt was evident in his expression.

"I changed my mind."

"Oh," Charles said. "I don't care where we have it, long as I get to marry this beautiful woman." He placed his arms around Lina and hugged and kissed her.

"Well, it doesn't matter to me either. I don't care if the wedding is in Timbuktu, I'll be there with bells on. I've never seen my nephew this happy."

Lina gave India a tight smile but didn't comment. She waited a few moments and then looked at her watch, making a gesture, feigning surprise.

"Is everything alright?" India asked, no longer ignoring Lina's sudden attitude change.

"Yes, everything's fine. I just remembered I have a huge photoshoot tomorrow and I haven't prepared for it."

"I'll let y'all go," India said. "I don't mess with nobody's money. Besides, we can get together again. You have to look over me because I'll mess around and keep you here all night, running my mouth about nothing and everything all at the same time."

Charles looked at his watch and then at his aunt. "I guess we should get on down. He stood and turned to Lina. "Baby, are you ready to get out of here?"

"I'm sorry, I wasn't trying to break up the visit. We can stay longer if you want."

"Nah, we need to get back to the city. He walked over to India and gave her a hug. I'll call you later."

After saying their goodbyes, Charles followed Lina out to the car. He pressed the unlock button on his key fob. Lina opened the door and jumped inside. Charles turned back to India who was standing in the doorway watching, and shrugged his shoulders. He didn't know what the reason was behind Lina's sudden change but he was sure he was about to find out.

Lina sat in the car shaking her foot. She was both angry and disappointed in Charles. She glanced out the window and noticed India waving. Lina waved back and then turned her head. She stared straight out the front window as Charles pulled off down the street.

"Baby, when did you decide you want the wedding in Durham?" Charles hoped talking about the wedding would lighten Lina's mood.

"I decided earlier today after talking to my mom. I was going to tell you when you came to pick me up but you were in such a rush to get to India's house it slipped my mind. Not that it really matters because there may not even be a wedding."

"What do you mean there may not be a wedding?" Charles maneuvered the car over, turning into a grocery store parking lot. He parked as far away from other vehicles as possible, giving him and Lina added privacy. "Lina, what's going on? What exactly happened in the bathroom because you were fine before you went in there? I've never seen you behave like this."

"You've never seen me behave like this? Well, I never thought the man I love and agreed to marry would betray me."

"What are you talking about?" Charles was beginning to develop an attitude of his own.

"I'm talking about you bringing me all the way out here pretending like you wanted me to meet your favorite aunt, when all along it was a set up. I guess you wanted the two little HIV ladies to have a play date."

Charles dropped his head. He wanted to defend himself but he wrestled with trying to figure out how Lina knew he'd told India about her condition. "Baby, that's ridiculous."

"Is it ridiculous, Charles? Let's see here, you tell me I have to meet your favorite aunt because she's like a *sister* to you." Lina stressed the word sister while making air quotes with her hands. "I'll bet it was killing the two of you when I was taking so long to use the restroom. I'm sure while I was in there you talked about how fun it would be when I came out and said something about India being infected. What did you think? I would come out and give her a big hug like we were at some type of support group? Whose idea was it for her to leave her medication on the vanity? Yours or hers? It was obvious she wanted to make sure I saw it."

"Baby, that's not what happened. Let me explain."

"Oh, I can't wait for this part. I'm sure you have an elaborate explanation already prepared. Did you memorize it or will you be reading it off index cards?"

"Lina, you're being unreasonable. Please...just hear me out."

"Say what you have to say and then take me home."

Charles turned to Lina. Although she wouldn't look at him, he focused his gaze on her. "Lina, I won't lie. When you shared your story with me about having HIV and how you got it I put up a good front while I was in your presence. Once I was alone, I was able to be free with my emotions. All I knew was that I loved you but I didn't know if I could accept all of the things that went along with being with someone who is HIV-positive. I know I promised you I wouldn't tell anyone, and I'm sorry I betrayed your trust. There was literally no one else I could feel comfortable talking to other than India. I knew she could give me the best advice and never judge you."

Lina turned to Charles with tear-filled eyes, "So that's why you chose to be with me? Because your auntie told you to?"

"No. Lina, that's not what happened. The only advice India gave me was to put myself in your shoes and follow my heart. Whether I chose to stay or go, the decision was mine alone. India didn't interfere at all. Her desire to meet you and me wanting you to meet her was all genuine. Everything I said about you meeting her was true."

"I guess next you're going to tell me you had nothing to do with the medicine in the bathroom."

I had absolutely nothing to do with it. I believe it was an honest mistake. India is always careful to keep her meds out of sight. What I don't understand is why you're so upset."

"I'm upset because I felt ambushed. I have no idea how many more people you've told. For all I know your entire family could know, and possibly your coworkers, too."

"I wouldn't do that to you, Lina. India is the only person I've told. I have no reason to lie."

"So, is marrying me some kind of pity party you're having? Am I your idea of community service in honor of your aunt? Are you trying to prove a point?"

"Lina, I love you. I loved you before I knew. Once you told me, my love for you didn't end. I don't know any other way to say it. I can't make you marry me but I will say, if you walk away you'll be leaving behind a man that truly loves you and would give his life for you."

Chapter Thirty

"Are you sure this is what you want to do, Lina?" Cheri asked, wiping tears from her best friend's eyes.

"Yes, I'm sure," Lina replied, nodding. "My tears are not those of sadness. I'm crying because I know I'm making the right decision for me, and the best part is, I'm doing it without the opinions or desires of anyone but myself."

"You're my best friend, Lina, and I love you." Cheri turned Lina toward her. "Now, the same as always, I have your back and I'm here for you through thick and thin. The only thing left for us to do is to get through this, and I know without a doubt you'll dominate this just like you have everything else in your life." Cheri wrapped her arms around Lina and held her tight. Seeing Lina in tears overwhelmed her heart. She fought back tears of her own.

"Cheri, don't you start crying, because if you get started I'll never stop," Lina chastised.

"It's not my fault. You started it. You're going to make me a sobbing mess. I cannot be looking crazy when I go out here and hook up with my man."

"I'm sure David has seen you looking more of a mess than this," Lina teased, evoking laughter from both of them.

Zarion tapped on the large wooden door before letting herself in. She looked at her sister and felt the sting of tears in her own eyes. "Sissy, you're so beautiful both inside and out. I'm so glad you made this decision. I came to get you because it's time to go. They're ready for us."

The three ladies stepped out of the room and met Lina's parents in the hall. Melodic tunes from the pipe organ filled the church, signaling the start of the ceremony. One by one, Lina's bridesmaids and their escorts walked down the aisle. The doors closed and the officiant asked the guests to stand.

Dun dun da dun… The doors parted and Lina stood at the back of the church with her mother on her left and her father on her right. As the organist played *Here Comes the Bride*, with slow, deliberate steps, Lina, and her parents, moved to the front of the church where Charles stood anxiously awaiting his bride.

The room was filled with joyful tears as Charles and Lina declared their love for each other and made vows before God to be faithful and to continue their love for the rest of their lives. Javonne approached the mic and serenaded the couple with a romantic ballad. The officiant asked both sets of parents to join Lina and Charles at the altar for a prayer of unity.

"By the power vested in me by the State of North Carolina, I now pronounce you husband and wife. Charles, you may kiss your bride." The guests erupted in laughter and applause when Charles dipped Lina and kissed her for the first time as man and wife. Once the applause ceased, the officiant asked Charles and Lina to turn and face the crowd. Extending his arms, he said, "I present to you Mr. and Mrs. Charles Davenport."

Charles took Lina by the hand and led her out of the church, followed by their bridal party and guests.

Photographers and the videographer swooped in, capturing timeless images. The love shared between Charles and Lina was unmistakable.

The wedding planner grabbed the couple and urged them to move on from the church to the reception venue. Upon arriving at the lush garden estate, the couple was greeted once again by their friends and family.

Lydia Fairweather kept her promise to give her daughter the most elaborate wedding imaginable. No expense had been spared from Lina's five thousand dollar wedding gown to the fifteen-thousand dollar reception. She wanted to spend more, but Lina protested.

The beautiful garden estate was elegantly decorated and offered plenty of space for the couple and their guests to dance the night away. The gift table overflowed with everything from large boxes to greeting cards. The plated dinner offered guests the choice between prime rib, chicken, and vegan options. At the conclusion of the evening, Lydia had arranged for a firework show that rivaled the fourth of July.

Charles looked into the eyes of his wife and swelled with pride. He covered her mouth with his for a slow, sensual kiss. "Sweetheart, you have always been the most beautiful woman I have ever seen. I didn't know it was possible, but you are more beautiful today than I could have ever imagined. I'm honored to be your husband. I love you, Mrs. Davenport."

"I love you, too, Mr. Davenport, and I'm honored to be your wife. I'm sorry your sister is not here. I know with all this joy you're also feeling the sadness of her absence."

"I won't lie, I'm disappointed, but I can't let it get to me. We tried all we could to get in contact with her. We all tried--me, you, my parents, and India. When Kellis is ready to be seen, she'll show up. Until then, I continue to pray the Lord will keep her safe and help her to make the right decisions."

Lina placed her hand on Charles' cheek. "It'll work out, baby." She dropped her voice an octave and spoke in a seductive tone. "It's been a long day. Unlike last night, tonight I'm your wife. I say, it's time to go."

Charles stepped back from Lina and bit his bottom lip. He lifted her arm and turned her around in a full circle, slowing down when his eyes landed on the back of her gown. Nodding his approval, he whispered in her ear, "Let's go."

After bidding farewell to their guests, Lina and Charles left to make their marriage official.

The newlyweds arrived at the 21c Museum Hotel by limo. Lina stood with amazement as she examined the unique artwork displayed within the hotel. "Charles, this place is absolutely beautiful. I can't believe I've never been here."

"It's nice to know I can take you places that you've never been, even in your hometown." He guided her through the chic modern designed lobby to the elevators. They boarded the elevator and Charles pressed the number fifteen.

"We're going to the top floor?" Lina asked, filled with excitement."

"Only the best for my bride." Charles leaned down and planted another kiss on her lips. The doors parted, giving them access to the 21c suite. The curtains were open, revealing breathtaking views of downtown Raleigh.

Lina kicked off her shoes and ran around the suite familiarizing herself with the place where she would give herself fully to her husband. Pushing the doors to the terrace open, Lina smiled with delight at the outdoor soaking tub. She turned around and found Charles standing behind her smiling.

"I take it, you like this room. It appears I made a good choice."

Lina looked back at the tub and then at Charles. "You made a great choice. How about we start here?"

"It would be my pleasure, but first, let's get you out of that dress." Charles pulled Lina inside and slowly undressed her. He playfully removed every string, button, and zipper. He kissed her neck, shoulders, and back as the dress fell to the floor. Lifting her out of the garment, he admired her bridal undies. "Um, um, ummm. Baby, you are so beautiful. I can honestly say, you were worth the wait." He reached out to grab her but was halted when Lina placed her hand on his chest.

"Not so fast, husband. I'm sure I've waited for this moment a lot longer than you have. You've unwrapped your gift. Now it's time for me to unwrap mine."

Lina and Charles explored one another's passions until they were both spent. Lying uninhibited in each other's arms, they vowed to never let anything or anyone come between what they had. Satisfied with their endeavors, they slept peacefully until the phone rang.

Chapter Thirty-One

Kellis stood on Charles and Lina's front porch completely unrecognizable. A long, wavy blond wig cascaded down her back, stopping at her waist. Large sunglasses covered her face from her forehead to her cheeks. She was covered in a t-shirt two sizes too big, and a pair of jeans.

Charles answered the door in complete surprise. She had phoned him from an unknown number and told him she was on her way to his house. He opened the door and would have closed it without question until she whispered his name. Recognizing his sister's voice, he stepped aside and allowed her to come inside. Stunned by her appearance, Charles almost tripped over the suitcases that set by the front door. He and Lina had just arrived home from their honeymoon in Italy and hadn't taken the time to unpack.

Kellis followed the familiar route to his living room and peeked out the windows before taking a seat.

Charles stood across the room from her with his arms folded. "Are you going to tell me what's going on or do I have to try to pull it out of you? And what is this disguise you're wearing. You look horrible."

"Thanks a lot, Charlie," Kellis replied, snapping her neck. She removed the glasses from her face and sat back against the sofa chair. "I'm sorry I wasn't at your wedding.

You know how it is."

"Don't patronize me. I know you didn't come over here to talk about the wedding. What's going on with you?" Charles stood firm, refusing to take a step closer to his younger sister.

"Charlie, I'm in trouble. I mean real trouble, big-time."

"What kind of trouble? Is there someone hurting you?" Softening, Charles stepped closer.

"I wish it were that simple then I would stand a chance. My troubles go much deeper."

Concern replaced Charles' anger. "Tell me everything and don't leave anything out."

"Can I get something to drink first? It's hot out there and I'm really thirsty."

"Kellis."

"I'm serious, Charlie. Can you please bring me a bottle of water or something to drink?"

Charles went to the kitchen and grabbed a bottle of water for his sister and one for himself. He returned and sat down, waiting for her to speak without prompting.

Kellis removed the top from the bottle and consumed half of the contents. "You know me and Bo have been together for a while now." She watched as Charles rolled his eyes at the mention of her boyfriend's name. "You don't have to do all that, Charlie. I know you don't like him."

"Get to the point, Kellis," Charles said, feeling his anger returning.

"This dude name Dirk was bothering me. He was constantly hitting on me, trying to get me to talk to him. I told him I had a man but he didn't care, he just kept on. One day he grabbed my arm and it pissed me off. I told Bo about it. Bo was like, don't even worry about it because he was gon' handle it. A couple days later, Bo asked me where Dirk hangs out."

Kellis paused, taking another sip from her bottle of water. "I told him I'll do him one better. We got in my car and I drove him over to where Dirk hangs out. When we got over there Bo confronted him. One thing led to another and Bo shot him. Bo jumped in the car and I sped off."

"Why in the world would you do something like that, Kellis? You know better. You've been playing this little hood chick game for way too long. The street life ain't nothing to play with. You see where it got me back in the day. Out here trying to be a little drug dealer got me two years locked down in juvie. Thank God I was a minor and the record was expunged, otherwise I may have never been able to rebuild my life. Now you're headed down the same path, except for you it'll be jail, if not prison. Have you been over to Mama and Daddy's house? We probably need to get together and send you off somewhere."

"I can't go to Mama and Daddy's house."

"What? Why not?"

"That's what I'm trying to tell you, Charlie. Somebody on Dirk's block snitched. The police already got Bo, and now they're looking for me. They would have already gotten me, but a couple of my friends hid me until you made it home. Why else would I be dressed like this?" Kellis said, pointing at her outfit.

Charles stood to his feet and stepped away from his sister like he would catch a charge by simply being in her presence. "You're a fugitive?" His heart sank.

"Charlie, they're talking about giving me twenty years because Dirk died. They're saying I was an accessory because I drove Bo over there. They offered him a deal if he gave them my name, and he did, Charlie. He took the deal." Kellis held her face in her hands and wept.

Charles rubbed his forehead back and forth as if he would rub up a solution. "Do Mama and Daddy know?"

"I don't think they know everything, but they do know the police are looking for me."

"You have really messed up this time, Kellis. I tried to warn you. We all did, but you wouldn't listen, now look. There's no way around this. You have to turn yourself in."

"You don't understand. I can't turn myself in, Charlie. I can't go to jail."

"You can't live a life on the run. For one thing you're broke and I'm not going to jail for aiding and abetting a fugitive. You made this bed, Kellis, now you have to deal with the consequences."

"Why are you acting like this? You're my big brother. You're supposed to look out for me. I'm telling you, I can't go to jail."

"I *am* looking out for you. If you turn yourself in at least we'll know you're safe. We'll get you a good attorney to represent you. I can't leave it up to chance and have you end up the next victim of an overzealous police officer."

"Charlie, listen to me, please." Kellis cried harder. "I can't go to jail."

"It'll be okay. You'll get through this." Charles reached for his phone.

Kellis stood and lifted her shirt. "Charlie, I'm pregnant. I can't have a baby in jail and I'm too far along to have an abortion. If I go to jail what's going to happen to my baby?"

Charles opened his hand, causing his phone to crash to the floor.

Epilogue

Lina tapped her foot nervously. At any moment she would become a mother. For months she and Charles made preparations to welcome their new addition. Her heart broke for her sister-in-law when the judge sentenced her to eighteen years in prison without parole. Charles apologized repeatedly for turning her in, but he felt he had no other option.

Kellis accepted her fate, and asked Lina and Charles if they would take her child and raise it as their own. Having no medical care prior to going to prison, Kellis didn't know how far along she was or what her baby's gender would be. She refused to bond with the baby in-utero because she felt she could never be a mother to the child. She gave her brother and sister-in-law one condition to the adoption. They had to agree to never tell the child she was the birth mother while she was still in prison.

Charles and Lina initially denied her request, saying it wasn't fair to Kellis or the child. She told them she didn't want the child to grow up knowing the woman who had given birth to him or her was incarcerated. With their continued refusal, Kellis threatened to have the baby adopted by an anonymous family in a closed adoption. Neither Charles nor Lina could live with the decision Kellis had made so they agreed to her terms.

Sitting in the waiting room of the prison hospital, they

anxiously awaited the arrival of their son or daughter. Lina chose to decorate the nursery in neutral tones until after the birth of the baby. She had always wanted to be a mother, but felt it was impossible due to her medical condition. Although she hated how things had occurred, she saw the baby as being her miracle and promised Kellis she would treat the child as such.

"Mr. and Mrs. Davenport," a tall brunette wearing a gray pantsuit called out from the entrance of the waiting room.

Charles and Lina jumped to their feet and stepped over to her. "We're the Davenports," Charles said, grabbing Lina by the hand.

The woman nodded. "My name is Miss Wittington. I'm the social worker here at the prison. Any correspondence you have received concerning your sister's pregnancy would have come from my office. I called you here to inform you your sister delivered a healthy baby this morning. The child weighed in at six pounds and seven ounces. I'll assume you came prepared with a car seat to take the child home with you today."

"Yes, we did," Charles said. "How is my sister? Can we see her?"

"Your sister is doing fine. Unfortunately, we don't allow inmates to receive visitors after giving birth. Prison rules. She will be returned to general population tomorrow, at which time you may adhere to the normal visitation schedule."

"Did she at least get to hold the baby?" Lina asked, showing concern for Kellis.

"No, ma'am. The inmate chose to have no contact with the child."

"You keep saying the child. I realize my sister is in prison, but the baby is not. Can you at least tell us if we have a niece or nephew?"

"Mr. Davenport, I know this must be difficult for you. However, you must realize your sister is here for a crime she committed. As for the child. I feel it will be in your best interest to not refer to the infant as your niece or nephew. You, your wife, and sister have completed the paperwork for the adoption of the child. The way I see it, you are this child's parent. I apologize for not revealing the gender. Give me one moment please." Ms. Wittington flipped through a manila folder, causing a chill to run down Lina's spine. "Mr. and Mrs. Davenport. You have a daughter."

"Welcome home, Micaela Kellis." Lina removed the baby from her car seat and snuggled her close to her heart. Charles busied himself, making several trips to the car removing bags of baby girl clothes, shoes, bedding, and toys. He'd suggested they come home first and shop the following day, but Lina insisted on making Micaela's nursery as girly as possible her first night at home.

Charles placed the shopping bags in the nursery and joined his wife and daughter in the living room. Sweetie sat on the floor near Lina's feet. Charles took a seat on the couch close to Lina. He peered down at the baby girl. "Wow, baby, she looks just like Kellis."

"Yes, she does. Your sister blessed us with a beautiful daughter."

"I know technically I'm supposed to say she's my daughter, but I can't see myself taking that title away from Kellis."

"Baby, we didn't agree to raise Micaela as a way of

taking her from Kellis. Your sister's desire to have us raise this beautiful baby girl as our own was a huge sacrifice for her. She didn't make the decision for us, she made it for Micaela. When I look at this precious baby, my instinct is to love and protect her. Kellis wants the same thing."

Lina lifted the baby and placed her in Charles' arms. "For the sake of your sister, and this precious gift we've been blessed with, I need you to recognize her as your daughter. We all do."

"I know you're right, sweetheart. It's just difficult." Charles leaned down and kissed the baby on top of her head. "I can't believe I'm a daddy."

"That's right, and you know what they say about a daddy's girl—she loves her daddy to the core." Lina held out her right hand, displaying the ring she received from her father and wiggled her fingers. "The bond between a father and his daughter is unbreakable."

The End

Note from the Author

Thank you for taking the time to read my 8th published work, *Lina's Redemption*. This book was truly a labor of love. Readers first met Lina Fairweather in *Positive Deception*, book one of the First Lady series. Lina's story was so profound to me because she suffered with an affliction that is quietly affecting millions of men and women, both young and old. Unfortunately, many of the victims of this illness suffer in silence. They feel their hope is lost and that they will never have a quality life. Writing *Lina's Redemption* was important to me because I want to share with others no matter what you're going through there is hope. God has a plan for your life and despite what it looks like right now, greater is coming.

The last line of this story is "The bond between a father and his daughter is unbreakable." Although the word used in the story is daughter, the statement is true whether you're a man or woman, boy or girl. John 3:16 (NIV) reads: *For God so loved the world that He gave his one and only Son, that whoever believes in him shall not perish but have eternal life.* God loves you, and He is concerned about the things that concern you. It doesn't matter what you've done or who you are, there is nothing you have done that will change God's love for you. Be confident and take comfort in the Word of God. Romans 5:8 (**NIV**) reads *But God demonstrates his own love for us in this: While we were still sinners, Christ died for us.*

Whether this is the first book you have read written by me or if you're an avid reader of my books, I want you to know you are loved and appreciated. My daily prayer is that the books I write will touch you in some way, be it entertainment or ministry. Your support does not go unnoticed and it is very much appreciated.

Once again, thank you for reading *Lina's Redemption*. I hope you enjoyed it. If you did, and would like to help support the series, the best thing you can do is leave a review at Amazon, Goodreads, or even your personal blog. Reviews help other readers determine if a series is to their liking, and authors rely on such word of mouth to get our books in front of new readers.

You can also sign up for my email newsletter at http://bit.ly/LAmailing⬚. The list receives no more than one or two emails per month, with updates on my next book, as well as recommendations of other authors you might like.

Questions for Discussion

1. Do you feel Lina was truly over Maxwell? Why or Why Not?

2. Were Lina's thoughts about her condition justified, or do you feel she was overreacting?

3. What is your opinion of Lina and her mother's relationship?

4. Was Charles wrong to make Lina wait three days? Why or Why Not?

5. Was Lina's anger justified when she and Charles left India's house? Why or Why not?

6. Did Charles make the right decision when he found out what Kellis had done? Why or Why not?

7. Do you know someone who struggles with the affliction Lina has? If so, how do you encourage that person?

8. How would you react to finding out someone you know has the same affliction as Lina?

Your Personal Invitation

Behold, I stand at the door and knock. If anyone hears My voice and opens the door, I will come in to him and dine with him, and he with Me. Romans 3:20 NKJV

As we go through life, we often seek ways to fill void areas in our hearts. Whatever you may be seeking, you can find it in a personal relationship with Jesus Christ.

If you believe God is knocking on the door of your heart, this is your opportunity to welcome Him into your life.

If you have never accepted Jesus Christ as your personal Lord and Savior, I extend to you this invitation.

About the Author

LaCricia A'ngelle is a licensed evangelist, author, and publisher. A native of Chicago, she currently resides in Georgia with her family.

To arrange signings, book events, speaking engagements, or to send comments to the author please email her at:
author@lacriciaangelle.com

Connect with LaCricia A'ngelle online at:
http://www.lacriciaangelle.com/
http://www.facebook.com/lacriciaangelle or
http://www.facebook.com/authorlacricia
Twitter: @authorlacricia
Instagram: @lacricia_angelle

Check out these awesome reads by
Author LaCricia A'ngelle

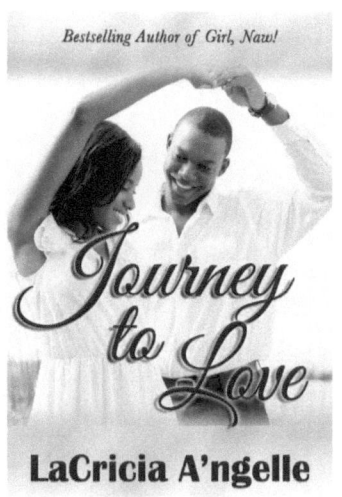